FIRST SPRING GRASS FIRE

Rae Spoon

FIRST SPRING GRASS FIRE

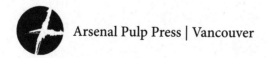 Arsenal Pulp Press | Vancouver

ARSENAL PULP PRESS
Suite 101, 211 East Georgia St.
Vancouver, BC V6A 1Z6
Canada
arsenalpulp.com

The publisher gratefully acknowledges the support of the Canada Council for the Arts and the British Columbia Arts Council for its publishing program, and the Government of Canada (through the Canada Book Fund) and the Government of British Columbia (through the Book Publishing Tax Credit Program) for its publishing activities.

Cover illustration by Elisha Lim
Book design by Gerilee McBride
Editing by Brian Lam
Author photograph by J.J. Levine
Printed and bound in Canada

Library and Archives Canada Cataloguing in Publication

Spoon, Rae
        First spring grass fire / Rae Spoon.

Issued also in electronic format.
ISBN 978-1-55152-480-1

        I. Title.

PS8637.P66F57 2012   C813'.6   C2012-904419-9

MIX
Paper from
responsible sources
FSC® C103214

For my sister and my brothers

Thanks to Oliver Fugler, Ivan E. Coyote, Sandhya Thakrar, S. Bear Bergman, Zoe Whittall, Shannon Webb-Campbell, Elisha Lim, Brian Lam, Dawn Loucks, and everyone at Arsenal Pulp Press.

Contents

Billy Graham

THE FIRST STADIUM CONCERT I ever went to was a Billy Graham rally at the Saddledome when I was nine. I remember taking the C-Train in from the suburbs with my family. For those of you who haven't been to Calgary, the Saddledome is a hockey arena shaped like a saddle. I had good memories of it because when I was younger I won contests in Sunday school memorizing and reciting books of the Bible and was rewarded with tickets to Calgary Flames hockey games. I was excited, but the ice and the Flames were gone, temporarily replaced by AstroTurf, a large stage of risers, and a portable wooden cross. I consoled myself with the fact that I got to wear white corduroy pants instead of a dress, a small victory in my losing battle against wearing my little sister's hand-me-down ruffles since she had already outgrown me by the time I was four.

That night ran like clockwork for an evangelical event. Praise and worship, a sermon, and an altar call to those who were lost to become born again and give their lives to Jesus. Some might have strayed from the faith and needed to recommit themselves, something I called "born again again."

Anyway, it wasn't the type of night I would have ordinarily remembered. Being raised with evangelistic fervor all around me, Pentecostal antics were normalized. At any moment in church, someone could start speaking in tongues (which sounds like a string of gibberish to a non-believer, but is thought to be the holy spirit speaking through people), and even at that age I had already seen several people slain in the spirit (when a person spontaneously falls backwards as a result of being overwhelmed by God). These events didn't impress me much, nor did the sight that evening of thousands of people streaming out of their seats in the bleachers to march wet-eyed onto the neon green artificial grass to get a closer look. I was shifting in my chair, counting the seconds on my plastic wristwatch, trying not to panic against the indeterminate ending of soul-saving events. I had come close to calming myself down just as Billy Graham stopped singing. Looking out over the crowd around the stage, he exclaimed, with sweat pouring down his face and a tremor in his voice, that heaven was going to be exactly like this meeting, like church, only it would never end. It would go on for eternity.

This was the beginning of doubt for me. I was nine years old and the best option that'd been presented to me was an eternity of Christian contemporary music. My imagination protested. My mind was full of places in books where people didn't have to wait for the school bus with numb legs in the cold all week just to spend the weekends inside of a church imagining hellfire. I begged internally for the option of non-existence.

I would stare at the slivers of the Rocky Mountains that I could see from my bunk bed and imagine crawling over them like they were tiny pebbles to the ocean. I would look into the clouds for messages that confirmed my doubts and find nothing—just a huge, God-filled sky over the dry grass on Nose Hill, brown after the snow melted and waiting for a lit cigarette to set the first spring grass fire.

Rushed Salvation

BEFORE MY FATHER'S DIPLOMA in computer programming allowed him to jump from construction work to an office job, we lived in the Calgary neighbourhood of Tuxedo Park, which was comprised of rows and rows of nearly identical townhouses. Each month my mother would walk with my sister Karen and me to a house at the furthest end from ours in order to pay the rent. Inside there was a man who had an office set up in his living room. It was dark with brown carpets and smelled of cigars. I loved the smell of cigar smoke. It reminded me of my favourite aunt's mobile home, only more fragrant.

Our home in Tuxedo Park was the first place where my sister and I could walk outside and away from our parents on our own. All of the backyards faced in, but had no fences between them. This shared green space allowed the neighbourhood parents some illusion of safety as we children could at least be kept away from the busy street while we played. There was the time when one of the other kids sold us a mud pie for nickel, which my sister and I somehow mistook for chocolate. We learned further about the harshness of life when we woke up one morning to find that someone had ripped the new tassels and twirlers off our pink bikes and thrown them in the dumpster (probably the same kid who sold us the mud pie).

From the age of two onward, we were not allowed to take off

any of our clothes outside of our bedroom, not even our shirts, because we were girls. The difference between a girl's chest or a boy's chest was hard for me to see then, so I sometimes forgot. I was once punished for wearing only the bottom of my bikini while I played swimming pool on my parents' waterbed. But I remember two specific times when I was allowed to bypass the strict rules.

Once, I peed my pants at daycare and got to wear boys' underwear from the lost-and-found; I was so happy about it that I refused to take them off at home and even wore them to bed. They felt better than the ones I usually got to wear that had flowers all over them. Then there was the time when I was four and got stung by a bee in the backyard. I remember feeling a sharp pain in the side of my neck and running howling into the house, and then having it explained to me that I had been stung. I got to spend the rest of that day with my shirt off, including lunch with my family. Secretly thrilled about it, I sat up tall in my chair. Otherwise, my little sister and I were usually dressed in matching pink outfits. We also had long, light brown hair, which we kept rolled in rags as we slept so we would have ringlets for family photos or church.

I very much identified as the older sibling to Karen when we were children. When she was born, I noted her inferiority to me (she couldn't even talk), so I took her in. I tried to teach her everything I knew, which included a repertoire of songs made by banging pots and pans, how to use colourful felt markers as makeup, and strict habits of self-control that had her potty-trained at a very early age. I once even upset all the parents waiting in a lineup with their children to see Santa when I turned to Karen, who was scared, and said, "Don't cry. It's just a man in a suit."

So when my mother came to me one night when I was four and told me that Karen had just given her heart to Jesus, I was appalled. It made no sense to me that she could be capable of doing something like this before me. After all, wasn't I the eldest? So I too was born again that night. I answered a series of questions my mother asked, which were meant to determine if I was old enough to understand my own mortality. I did so by kneeling next to her and repeating, "Yes. I know I was born a sinner. Yes, I understand that Jesus died for my sins. Yes, I want to live my everlasting life with Him. Yes, I will devote my life to the service of His will."

But what I was really focused on was catching up with my sister. If this meant that she was going to get to meet Jesus before me, I would have to figure out how to spiritually accelerate in order to pass her in the race. So I guess the way I officially joined the church was a simple case of sibling rivalry.

After that, I was more watchful of her to make sure that she didn't do anything to encroach on my position. It wasn't often an issue, though, because she befriended other children while I preferred to talk to ants. When I would be in my room playing guitar quietly to myself, she would be dancing around hers to a *Dance Mix '92* cassette with her friends. Even when we shared a room with L-shaped bunk beds, it didn't look like we were going to end up in the same universe. She was the girl that my parents wanted us both to be, and I was trying to lay low and get away with acting like a boy as much as I could.

In grade twelve I made my girlfriend tell Karen that we were dating while I shivered in the next room because I was so scared she would shun me for being gay. She was one of the last people we came out to. Three months later, I got the shock of my life when she herself came out to us. We all went to the same high school, where word got around; our basement was rumoured to be a lesbian love dungeon. Like being born again, my sister and I experienced the homophobic hatred together, sometimes evading carloads of boys together and running defense to make sure our family didn't find out we were queer. In those spaces, I can't see myself as separate from her. We managed it all together. I am able to admit now that Karen beat me to salvation, but we escaped our religious heritage together.

1988

FOR CHRISTMAS IN 1987, I got two presents from my parents: a stuffed blue dinosaur and a large black Bible. Though I was only six, the latter made me feel incredibly grown up. It was bound in fake black leather, had gold embossed letters on the cover, and was cool to the touch. I would hold it close to my chest and carry it around the house. My favourite thing about it was the fact that everything Jesus said was written in red, the colour of blood. I would scan through the red passages to learn what I thought must be the most important information, since it came directly from the Son of God. As hard as I looked, though, there was never any mention of dinosaurs. Now that I think of it, it's amazing that my parents gave me that blue dinosaur; somehow it was exempt from their war on non-biblical creatures. It certainly fared better than the unicorn my sister got from someone on her fifth birthday; as soon as her party ended, my father took it to the bathroom and cut its horn off. From then on, it was just a horse with a hole in its forehead.

I went through a phase in which I was obsessed with dinosaurs. I memorized their names and special qualities like club tails, claws, or mouthfuls of teeth. It started with a class trip to the Royal Tyrrell Museum in Drumheller, where replicas of dinosaur skeletons were strung up from the ceiling. I could barely believe that these giant creatures had been pulled right out of the ground in Alberta. From then on, I would play endlessly with my plastic dinosaurs and look for fossils in our garden, convinced that I would find one some day. It seemed inevitable.

That same year, my family made room for the arrival of a new baby. My sister and I already had a brother, Craig, who was born in 1985. Jack was born on New Year's Day, 1988, at five in the morning. A few hours earlier, after we toasted the New Year at midnight with ginger ale and watched the big apple drop in Times Square on TV, our parents made their way to the hospital, leaving my sister, brother, and me with a babysitter. When we woke up, we found her sitting in the living room. "Guess what? You have a new baby brother!" she said as I rubbed my eyes awake. Our father took us to meet Jack at the hospital. On the way there I picked out his first present, a grey wrinkled dog puppet that was larger than him.

I was about to turn seven. Having three younger siblings had started to feel like being in command of a small army. When Jack came home I took on the role of helping to take care of him. I would change his diaper, feed him, sing to him. There is a picture of us four children just after he was born, taken on a Sunday before church. I am in a pink dress with a grin on my face holding Jack, who is dressed in a fancy sleeper. My sister Karen is standing on one side of me wearing a dress similar to mine, and our brother Craig is on the other side, dressed in a tiny suit with his wet hair combed down. I will never forget how proud I was to hold Jack by myself, feeling his weight in my arms as I cradled his neck and held him safely off the ground.

A month after Jack was born, the Winter Olympics came to Calgary. In art class, we had prepped for the entire school year beforehand. I must have drawn the Olympic rings a hundred times in scrawled pencil outlines that were then filled in with semi-accurate colours. The symbol for the Calgary Olympics was too difficult, being an intricate snowflake with cowboy boots on all of the tips.

The entire city was anxiously awaiting the Olympics, and I could feel it too. Every public school in Calgary was given a replica of the torch, complete with a plastic flame. One morning at our school, on one of the coldest days of the year, we were taken outside one classroom at a time so that each student could run around the field with it. When it was my turn, I remember panting down the snow-covered grounds with my legs and hands quickly turning numb, struggling to hold up the torch. It seemed very important. During the Games, the Calgary Tower, a prominent feature of the downtown skyline, had a gas-fuelled flame shooting out the top, turning it into the world's largest Olympic torch. We could see the flame on the tower from almost everywhere in the city. When Canadian Elizabeth Manley won the silver medal in figure skating, I saw a picture of her on the front page of the newspaper, biting down on it like a cookie. I asked my mother, "Why is she doing that?" My mother answered, "So she can see if it's real."

After two weeks, the Olympics came to an end, the flame on the tower was snuffed out, and the world receded from our doorstep. The snow melted and I resumed my hunt for fossils in our yard.

There were little sprigs of green coming up from underneath the grass that had been killed by winter's deep freeze, and the wind was blowing the loose dirt around like it always does in March.

Jack was two months old and getting bigger every week. Then one day while my mother was out shopping for glasses, he was napping and didn't wake up. She found him when she got home. Everyone else was watching television in the basement. Her scream sent my father barrelling up the stairs with all of us kids behind him. After the ambulance took my mother and Jack away, my father shuttled Karen, Craig, and me away from the house. I remember turning to my sister in the car and saying, " Don't worry, Karen. Jesus will save him."

The events that followed are like photographs. Most of them are blurry: the ambulance, my divorced grandmother and grandfather in the same room at the same time for the first time in my life, church people's casseroles, the funeral, and red, tear-stained adult faces everywhere. A lot of people I'd never met before.

Loss crashed in as clear as the glaring Alberta sunlight. I felt weightless. I had a refrigerator-box fort in the basement that I crawled into for the better part of three days. Unable to feel my body, I started to believe that there was no way that any of it was real. I would lie inside the box praying for a sign from God to show whether I was real or not, all the while clutching a yo-yo my aunt had bought for me.

Over the next few months, whenever I got upset, I was told that Jack was in heaven. It was the only information about where he might have gone to that I got from my parents, my teachers, and even my own friends. But I could never picture it. It seemed like the opposite of where we had put him. We got rid of his crib and his clothes and he started to disappear altogether. My family went to the graveyard only once after the funeral. Losing Jack was something we stopped talking about, and other things just started piling up on top of it. But it would come out in other ways. Once, years later, my father and I were playing marbles on the living room floor. We were both on our stomachs facing each other on the beige carpet. All of a sudden, my father said, "This is what death is like. God decides it's time and you are knocked out, gone. Like Jack." Then he struck a bunch of my marbles out. Life was a game that I had no control over. Between God and my father, almost everything was out of my hands. But the moment I realized I could sing and play guitar at the same time, I wrote a song about Jack. Songs became where I could put my secrets, my pain, and my little brother. They were in my head where no one could find them.

Many years later, my cousin Ben visited from Penticton. We were driving around in his car smoking and somehow we started talking about how Ben had never met Jack. Ben, being impulsive, insisted on driving me to the graveyard when I admitted that I hadn't been there since I was a child. I knew where it was, though, because I had passed it every day on the city bus to school when I moved to my grandmother's house for a while. I often thought about stopping there but never got off the bus.

We pulled up to the curb, hopped over the fence, and walked

into the graveyard. The ground was covered in snow. I looked all around me and realized there was no way I was going to figure out where Jack's headstone was. I started to feel weightless at the thought of not finding him. Tears welled up in my eyes. Then I felt a snowball hit my chest. It was Ben. "I bet the babies here never had a snowball fight!" he said. I grinned and filled my hands with snow. We ran around throwing snowballs at each other and laughing until we were out of breath. I had been carrying around two plastic dinosaurs in my pocket on and off since I was six. I felt them in the palm of my hand, scanned the graveyard, and said, "These are for you." I threw them as hard as I could, and then we walked back to the car and drove away.

Voyageur Girls

A LOT OF GIRLS JOIN the Brownies when they are young. Some of them are in it for the cookies and others like the outfits. My club, the Voyageur Girls, had one up on Brownies because it was endorsed by Jesus Christ and he was Lord of everything, including cookies.

I was nine when I joined. We would meet upstairs in our church on Tuesday nights. We started each session by sitting in a circle singing Christian songs, led by the wife of a heart surgeon who played acoustic guitar. Her daughters were too old for Voyageur Girls and her son was my age, but not allowed in. The theme song for the group was a biblical quote about how Jesus would guide us through life: "Thy word is a lamp unto my feet and a light unto my path. When I feel afraid and feel I've lost my way, you are there right beside me."

Singing with the other Voyageur Girls pulled me out of my aloneness. I didn't have many friends at school, and it was one of the rare group activities that I participated in where I wasn't mortified by the attention of others. At school, I was known to freeze up right before I was supposed to perform a jump or something in gym class if I sensed that someone was watching me.

After singing came craft time. We braided plastic bracelets, baked Fimo beads, and puffy-painted sweatshirts. I would covertly choose boy colours like blue and green and avoid the pinks and purples. Sometimes we coloured pictures of Jesus doing all sorts of things like making a lot of food out of a little bit, or raising people from the dead. We were made to believe that He was white, so the peach crayons always wore out before the others, as did the blue ones for His eyes. I didn't mind making crafts. I could keep my head down and work uninterrupted.

We would earn badges that we would then display on the blue sashes that we wore across our chests. The badges were earned mostly for domestic activities like cleaning and sewing, things girls needed to be good at. These gave me a sense of foreboding, and I started to wish that I would never grow up to become a woman and that I would stay a child forever. I knew that I was a girl, but I didn't feel like a girl. I had heard the term "sex change," but I ducked low on the playground and let it sail over me. It was a sin and an insult, after all. Voyageur Girls really blew my cover, though. In the absence of boys, I seemed even more boyish. The other girls could sense that I was different. They tried to be nice to me, just like we all never made fun of the girl named Gaylene. It wouldn't have been very Christian. That doesn't mean that we didn't say her name to ourselves quietly and giggle. I'm sure they giggled at the thought of me.

The last part of each Voyageur Girl meeting, though, was where I could truly shine, when we would read the Bible together. Anything that involved reading built my confidence. Week after week, I would proudly recite to the group leader a verse or chapter that I had memorized. In fact, I memorized so much that I got a special gold pin for it. None of the other girls had this pin. I displayed it proudly at the top of my sash.

At the end of my first year of Voyageur Girls I was managing to fly under the radar, unlike at school, where people would pick fights with me by calling me a tomboy. That is, until it was time for us to go to Voyageur Girls camp. Camp was an entire weekend of sharing bunk beds and bathrooms together in the woods. Though I protested, my parents made me go. They probably hoped that being around the other girls would rub off on me and that I would come home begging to wear dresses and clean the house.

So I got on the bus with the other Voyageur Girls on Friday afternoon and we arrived at the camp that night. I chose the top bunk because it gave me a vista. But I always had trouble with nightmares. Sometimes I would dream that my father's moustache was chasing me. That night I had another nightmare. In it my mother told me that I had to grow up and be a woman and get married in only ten minutes. I rolled right off of my bunk bed onto the floor. I woke up dazed and in the middle of yelling, "I won't wear a wedding dress!" Next thing I knew I was in the arms of one of the camp counselors. She had the same name as my mom. I was so embarrassed that it ached more than the bruises from the fall. By the morning, the story of my accident was all over camp.

At breakfast, I tried to hide behind my hair, but it didn't work as well as it usually did. I could feel eyes burning my face. I barely ate and then retreated alone to the corner of the room. For free time, some of the other girls gathered around the piano and played

"Heart and Soul" over and over and over as I watched. The melody repeated along with the following thought: *I'm not one of them. Now they know.*

And then I did the only thing I'd ever learned to do when I was feeling bad. I bolted, running breathlessly out the door and toward the forest, ignoring my fear of the woods. I looked desperately for a low branch on a tree that I could climb up, but there were only scraggly pines. Back home in the suburbs, I had spent many an afternoon hiding from being a girl in a tree.

Deeper inside the bush, I found a clearing. I decided to build a shelter. I began gathering branches, both large and small, and leaned the largest ones against each other so they balanced. Then I took the smaller branches and weaved them in between until my shelter looked like the lopsided back of a turtle. I knelt down and tore thick pieces of moss off the forest floor, which I used to plug up the spaces between the branches. The wood-and-moss dome I created was just big enough for my body. Once inside, I laid down on the cold ground. It was silent, like forests are. Only the sounds of birds and wind.

A while later I heard footsteps. It was the Voyageur camp leader who played the acoustic guitar. She had a big smile on her face. "What is this?" she asked.

"My fort," I whispered.

"What are you doing in there?" she asked.

"Hiding," I said.

She paused and knelt beside me. I laid my head down on the moss.

"You know that song we sing at Voyageur Girls? It means that God is always with you. So whatever you're hiding from, He can help you face it." I said nothing.

"It's almost lunch time," she said. "You should come back to the camp." Then I heard her steps recede as she walked away.

Why would God make me like this? I thought. *And where can I hide from growing up?*

Sasquatch in My Shower

THE FIRST MOVIE I EVER remember seeing was at a drive-in cinema on the outskirts of Penticton. I was about four at the time. I can determine that because my brothers hadn't been born yet, so it was just me and my sister and my parents in our silver Datsun. My uncle and his family were parked next to us, and our cousins ran back and forth between the two cars.

We covered our laps with a grey camping blanket and listened to the audio crackling on the car radio. The movie was called *Harry and the Hendersons*. It starts with the Henderson family driving down a road flanked by trees. An animal runs out in front of their car and they hit it with a sickening thud. In the silence that follows, they approach it but are shocked to find that it has huge human hands. They think it's dead, but don't want to leave it there, so they hoist it onto the roof rack of their station wagon and continue driving. Just as things seem to calm down, the animal comes back to life. It leans over the roof rack, sticks its face in the windshield, and lets out a roar. Even though Harry, who turns out to be a Sasquatch, eventually becomes a charming addition to the Henderson family, it's the sound of that roar that has stayed with me.

As a result, I developed a lifelong case of Sosantoglitaphobia, the fear of Sasquatch. Even though I camped a lot as a child, the woods are something I am most comfortable seeing on TV or out the window of a vehicle. Otherwise, there are too many things to worry about. Like getting grabbed by a mythical creature, for example.

After my brother Jack died when I was seven, I started having a series of recurring nightmares about a Sasquatch, but then one day he sneakily slipped from my subconscious and into my waking hours. My sister and I used to share a bedroom in the basement of a bungalow in Whitehorn, the third house we lived in. The room was at the bottom of the stairs down a hallway that went past the basement bathroom. I started to see the outline of what I thought was a Sasquatch behind the fogged glass of the shower whenever I walked past the bathroom. Because the basement was always dark, there was never a moment where I felt safe enough to venture into the bathroom and dispel my fears by opening the door. So the ominous image persisted. I could feel it watching me whenever I passed. I couldn't pretend that I wasn't scared, so I developed an evasive technique: I would fly from my room down the hall, past the bathroom, and then purposely run into the wall, so that I wouldn't have to slow down to turn before dashing up the stairs. I never told my mother about the Sasquatch in the shower. However, I remember her asking me once about the repeated thumps of my exit routine. I was a secretive child and didn't tell her why, but I think it led her to figure out that we were too young to live in the basement. My sister and I were moved upstairs into the room that used to be my brother Jack's. It was light in there all the time.

My parents decided to fill the empty room in the basement by inviting a pregnant teenager to live with us. They were avid pro-lifers and had found an organization that placed pregnant teens in Christian homes to encourage them to carry their babies to term. Only a few months after losing her own baby, my mother presumably wanted to feel like she was helping to keep babies alive.

So Stacey moved in. She was nineteen, mild mannered, and five months pregnant. I remember her eating dinner with us and helping my mother to cook, clean, and do laundry. I didn't understand why she had to live with us if she was so grown up. She slept a lot and made jokes about how her belly was making an indentation in the hide-a-bed in her room. My mother made her drink a lot of milk and seemed more relaxed than before. Then one night while I was sleeping, Stacey went into labour; soon after, she gave birth at the hospital. After that, she moved out and I never saw her again.

The second girl who came to live with us was named Rachel. She was fifteen, had bright red hair, and was two months pregnant. We picked her up at a group home downtown. My parents told me that she had been doing drugs and sex work. They said our home was a place for her to hide from her pimp who was angry she had left him and wanted to hurt her. I really liked Rachel. She acid-washed her jeans in our laundry room and tried to make handprints on them by pouring bleach over her hands. I thought she was cool. My parents weren't as impressed. Unlike Stacey, she refused to go to church with us the first Sunday morning she was there, and when we returned we noticed that the speakers in our stereo were blown out. That night when my father tried to talk to her about doing chores, she picked up a coffee table and threw it at him. The one time she came with us to church, she wore long dangling earrings and her acid-wash jeans, and sat slouched down in the pew.

The month that Rachel lived with us was full of outbursts. She didn't respond well to being coerced into polite Christian compliance. When we went to the mall, she took off when my mother wasn't looking. We finally found her hanging out with a group of men we didn't know. My parents pulled her away and then we all left for home. That afternoon there was a different commotion. My father walked Rachel out of the house doubled over. When they came back from the hospital, she was grey. My mother said, "Rachel had a miscarriage, but it was God's will and probably for the best." Rachel slept for a few days and then we took her back to the group home.

In the frenzy, I forgot all about the Sasquatch. When the house was quiet again, the form in the basement bathroom didn't return. My fears had moved out of the basement shower and into my chest. The death of my brother and now Rachel's miscarriage was too much for me. When I looked at our beige carpet in the living room or put a hand on our pink couch, I couldn't connect to them. Why did I feel completely alone if Jesus was in my heart? I would curl up and tell myself that I wasn't from here, that this couldn't be my world, and that I would be taken away to my real life soon.

While I waited, I threw myself into books, sometimes reading most of my waking hours. All I had to do was scan my eyes over the words and let them fill my mind. I would be transported somewhere else. In every other aspect of life, though, I felt like I was just going through the motions. I was a secret agent and infiltrator, but no one else knew. A few years later, I started writing stories. Each one felt like a small piece of the world I was building that I was eventually going to move into, one where babies didn't get taken away, and Sasquatches didn't exist.

Nerd Pride

THERE'S A PICTURE IN MY junior high yearbook that shows me in the middle of a line of kids holding onto a rope in a tug of war. I have a mushroom haircut and big glasses, and I'm smiling with new adult teeth I had yet to grow into. I am wearing a sweatshirt and light blue jeans that were pulled up as high as they could go, and a fanny pack cinched around my waist instead of a belt. I am pulling the rope earnestly as if I have no clue that I am not making much of a difference. This was the first day of junior high, the place where I found out that I was a nerd.

In my first homeroom I remember girls comparing their Doc Martens and hooded flannel vests that had become popular over the summer. I wondered why everyone wanted to wear the same thing as everyone else. My wardrobe came from my mother. I rarely tried to push for specific items, except for my covert attempts at wearing as close to boys' clothes as I could get away with. By then, the closest I had gotten to my own style was the year I dressed like Ernest P. Warrell, the character from TV and movies. I thought he was funny and hoped that by dressing like him, I would become funny too. I would wear a denim vest, jeans, a grey shirt, and a tan hat every day, and do my Ernest impression for my friend Kenny while we folded up pieces of paper into Vs to shoot with elastic bands at recess. He seemed to think that I was funny. But junior high was different. Those girls in homeroom never talked to me. I kept my distance, sitting with the other kids who were in band in the corner of the class. It was clear what we were going to be for the next three years.

During lunch hours I would eat with the band kids or walk around the schoolyard alone. I would wear my fanny pack full of stationery supplies, because I used to worry that I would need an eraser or something and not have one at my disposal. Sometimes I would eat my lunch and then pace around the halls watching the other kids talking to each other, never looking at them long enough to be noticed. I was trying to figure things out. They seemed to just find each other. *How did they find each other?*

At the first gym class I was horrified when I realized that we were going to have to change our clothes in a locker room. The other girls congregated next to the rows of beige lockers and talked about shaving their legs. I dodged into a bathroom stall. I could hear them all singing this song as I hid, pulling my T-shirt over my head. I think it went something like "I Will Always Love You." My Pentecostal parents had only ever let me listen to Christian music. *How did they all know that song?*

In gymnastics that day, I was on the parallel bars trying to keep myself up when I felt a hot, ripping pain in my chest. My arms gave out. I started crying, crumpled up on the floor. The gym teacher came over and said, "You're okay, you're not hurt," and pulled me to my feet. I could feel my face turn red. One of the other girls approached me with a big smile and said, "Hey, it's okay. I used to want to be a boy too." I felt the floor giving way underneath me.

That was the second time she'd gone out of her way to point out that I was bad at being a girl. She was onto me.

A week later, we began the dance aerobics portion of gym class. The boys were outside playing rugby, which looked violent, but not as horrible as trying to move around gracefully to music. I had never been allowed to dance in my life. My parents thought it was sinful. The pumping beat of "Rhythm is a Dancer" came on and the gym teacher started to call out moves and demonstrate them. "Grapevine!" I could feel my body resisting as I urged it to move to the music like a limp scarecrow. I knew that if I didn't dance I would be in trouble with the teacher, but if I did, I might go to hell. I thought I saw the gym teacher raise an eyebrow at me as I shimmied, feeling conflicted behind all the other girls who seemed to be having a genuinely good time. At the end of the class, the teacher said, "Good job, girls! Tomorrow you are going break up into groups and come up with your own routines."

That night when I was in the bath, I looked at my mom's pink razor. I grabbed it and turned it over in my hand. I could still hear the girls talking about their new bras in the locker room that day. I had to do something. I dragged the razor up my leg, shaving off the tiny blond hairs. But then I slipped and cut my knee. Blood dripped into the bath water. *Can't stop now*, I thought. I bit my lip and continued. Afterwards my mother saw my legs covered in cuts and said, "What happened to you?"

I hung my head. "I shaved my legs."

"But you're only twelve," she said. "You don't need to."

She didn't know how much I needed to do something that made me seem like a girl.

"Yes. I do!" I said.

"Well, did you use soap? Next time use soap." She patted my head and walked away.

In gym class the next day, no one noticed my attempts at becoming a woman. The teacher broke us into groups. "Come up with a routine to the song I give you," she said. Our group was assigned the particularly sinful song "Gonna Make You Sweat (Everybody Dance Now)." I had never heard the song before. We took our tiny stereo and went to a corner of the gymnasium.

"We should start in a line," one girl said, trying to take control, "and then we can wave our arms up and down like this. It will look like water!"

Kill me now, I thought.

Slowly our routine unfolded. It involved a lot of loosely choreographed manoeuvres which we tried to do in unison. We made the routine longer by doing our moves close to each other at first, and then further apart. By the end of the class I was certain that we had created a routine that would not only confirm how deeply flawed I was at being a girl, but also send me straight to hell, forever.

The next day it was show time. Other groups went up and managed to perform through waves of their own giggles. Suddenly it was our turn. I stood up and joined my group on the blue gym matt. My heart was racing. The gym teacher pressed play on our song, and we stood motionless in a line, waiting for the right note to kick in before starting the routine. As the synthesizer washed over us, something happened to me. Something far back in my mind snapped. *I can't do this*, I thought. A voice spoke to me. At that moment, I thought it was Jesus. It said one word: "Run!"

I bolted out of line and out of the room like someone had pulled a pin from a spiritual grenade. By the time the singer had started the chorus, I was halfway down the hallway. I had no idea where I was running.

After my near-dance routine experience, I gave up trying to understand my classmates. I had a new tactic: getting lost in outer space. I saw *Star Trek: The Next Generation* on television and became fascinated with both the series and the idea of space travel. The show provided an escape not only from junior high, but the entire world. After hearing Captain Picard reference quantum physics, I decided to look into them.

I started to spend my lunch hours in the library reading books about wormholes and antimatter. I would close my eyes and imagine the great darkness of outer space. Of course, life had been hard. I'd been looking at things that were too small. The things that were important weren't of this world. They were big, like God.

I came up with my own theory of the universe. I read that black holes might actually be wormhole gateways to another universe. As matter was pulled into them, it moved faster—so fast that at some point, time actually stopped. This point was known as the event horizon. I had read a theory that this was the point where the polarities on atoms switch, so when the object emerged in the new universe, it was antimatter. Eventually, I theorized, everything from our universe would be pulled into the other, antimatter side. Of course, beyond that was the spiritual realm of heaven, where God presided over the laws of physics.

I made a diagram of my theory on a poster board. My science teacher happened to be in the library one lunch hour and asked me to explain it to him. He nodded as I told him what each part meant. "That's great," he said, "but shouldn't you be doing other things on your lunch hour? I'm worried about you. This isn't normal."

I smiled and replied, "Don't worry about me. I like being here."

But when I found out that quantum physics involved math, I chucked away my whole theory and my preoccupation with it. I was never able to concentrate on numbers for long. My theory was not sound and would have been immediately disproven by anyone over the age of thirteen. Yet trying to come up with an explanation for where matter went through black holes was less daunting than getting along with the girls in my gym class. Those lunch hours that I spent imagining outer space allowed me some more time to grow up before I really had to interact with others. No one ever told me that being a nerd was okay, but I chose to embrace it like it was an appointment by God because it seemed like the only thing that I could do.

I Will Be a Wall

SIX MONTHS AFTER MY brother John was born, there was tension throughout our house. Everyone was uneasy with the fear that John would die like Jack had a few years earlier. It felt like we were waiting out his infant years more than we were enjoying them. One night during that time, my father stopped sleeping. He stayed up all night changing the combination-lock code on his briefcase and rustling around the house performing other mysterious rituals. I could hear his briefcase constantly clicking open and closed and the shuffle of his feet from one place to another. The next morning, with bags under his eyes, he took me aside and said, "Your mother is trying to kill us. She's putting poison in our food." But that night he ate his entire dinner while I stared at him from across the table, waiting for a cue.

For years he had been telling us that we were making him sick by kicking up dust in the house or that the world could end at any moment, but he would always do so in a cool, reasoned tone, and often out of the blue, like he was just recalling something he had forgotten that he wanted us to know. It never seemed like he thought it was an emergency, until he came up with the story of my mother's poison plot.

That same week, things started to happen in clusters, like a rain outside that you can't hear at first but which gets slowly louder until it's impossible to ignore. It started with my father buying flowers for my mother at the local grocery store. When I saw him come into the house with them, he said, "I bought these because I love your mother so much."

By the end of the week he was looking wild-eyed and shooting accusations at her. In the middle of it, I could hear the two of them fighting in their room right next to mine. My father opened my door and turned on the light. "Get up," he said. "We're going." I walked out of my room rubbing my eyes and saw that he had rounded up all three of my siblings. My sister was holding John, who was a baby, in her arms, in that way children hold babies, his feet barely off of the ground. Craig, who was seven, stood dazed next to them. "Your mother is trying to kill us," he said, and raced down the stairs to start the van.

I could hear her sobbing on the phone in the kitchen. I made it down to the landing just as he walked back into the house. His coat smelled like exhaust, the same way it always smelled when he got back from work in the winter or was puttering with the van in the garage. "Come on. Let's go."

I was between him and my siblings. I could hear my mother talking to my uncles, telling them to come and help us. I moved toward leaving with him and then stopped. My mother shouted at me across the house, "Don't leave with him. He's sick. He has schizophrenia."

I didn't really know what the last part meant, but there was something in the tone of my mother's voice that told me I should believe her. She didn't sound like she wanted to kill all of us. She was terrified of my father. We couldn't leave with him. I drew myself up and said, "We're not going with you."

At that moment I lost awareness of where or who I was. I was a wall with one job: to keep him away from them. I made myself look as big as I could for an eleven-year-old, and somehow he didn't push me out of the way. He just looked at me with hurt in his eyes and then left.

Fifteen minutes later, my uncles arrived at our house. We threw our backpacks into their trucks and piled into them. As we started to pull away, a police car turned up and my mother got out to talk to them. We then drove in silence to the east side of the city where my aunt lived. I looked out at the yellow dawn and tried to wrap my head around what had just happened. *My father is a schizophrenic? What's that?*

We camped out in our aunt's basement, and in the morning I picked at a fast food breakfast in front of a television that was way bigger than what I was used to. Later, I sat on the stairs out of sight and overheard everything my mother told my aunt. My father had been diagnosed with paranoid schizophrenia when he was sixteen. His family never told my mother and she only found out during their first year of marriage. *Why hadn't she told me?*

My mother got a restraining order against my father, but that Monday he accidentally turned himself in by going to the police station to report my mother's homicidal plans. The police saw the restraining order filed under his name and talked him into going to the hospital. They called us and we went outside for the first time since that Saturday night.

My father had returned to the house, where he had been alone for the last two days. I found a list of all the odd things he had done that my mother had typed for his psychologist. He had nailed the windows shut on the ground floor, blown off the top of the barbecue, and hidden glass shards under the door near the entrance as a crude trap. He had anointed a clay dinner bell, a present from his sister's missionary trip to Mexico, in olive oil and left his copy of the Bible open with two gloves facing up like praying hands on either side.

While my father was in the hospital, my mother went to visit him there every night, so we were left home alone a lot. After dinner my sister and I would put John and Craig to bed. In the living room, Karen and I were often convinced that someone was breaking into the house. We would huddle on the couch breathing nervously and listening for the sound of footsteps outside. Sometimes John would wake up screaming and I would have to try to calm him down. It was hard because I knew I wasn't the one he wanted.

My mother asked me told not to tell anyone about my father's illness or what had happened that awful weekend. He had just been elected deacon at our church and she didn't want him to have to resign. I couldn't concentrate at school and spent most of my time wondering if there was any truth in the things my father had said to me over the years.

The first time I visited my father in the hospital, we took an elevator up to the top floor. It was my sister's birthday. My mother told us a story about how she had come there the day before with the pastor from the church and he had cast some demons out of a female patient by putting his hand on her head. I believed her. When we walked into my father's room, he was sitting at a table with a pencil and a piece of paper checking off what he wanted to eat for dinner. He looked different; the wildness was gone from his eyes, but there was nothing there to replace it. He looked empty and docile. "The food's actually pretty good here," he said, marking off the boxes for toast, soup, and jello.

After he came home, he would sleep on the couch all day and struggle to pay attention for more than short periods of time. We all fell into a lull. My mother said he had been sick, but that he was getting better. I waited for the parts of him that I had liked before to come back.

Six months later he started going to meetings that were run by a fundamentalist Christian men's movement. He came home after one of their gatherings and called a family meeting. Looking at each one of us, he said, "Men need to take back their rightful place as spiritual leaders in their homes. That's why this country is falling apart. I am the man of this house and I need to take back my place as head of it."

That night I woke up to the sound of him shuffling around the house again; soon the accusations returned, and the wildness came back into his eyes. He had gone off his pills so he could be a stronger leader. I became a wall again. This time I watched him and when he started to slide, I situated myself between him and my siblings until he ended up back at the hospital and on his pills.

When I was thirteen, my mother claimed to be divorcing him after a particularly violent incident, but then let him move back into the house when he got out of the hospital. She always tried to tell me he was just sick, but I knew there was more to it than that. He was cruel to all of us, even when he was on his pills. She would waffle between agreeing with me when I brought it up and being loyal to him. He saw me as a traitor who had turned on him. Meanwhile, he again tried to reassert his authority over our family. Each night after dinner, he would make us stay at the table while he read long passages from the Bible and then made us all name a thing that we were thankful for.

After my mother found some of my writing in which I talked about suicide, there was an ongoing debate between my parents and me about which one of us was crazy. I was sent to a Christian therapist. My father often threatened to send me to the hospital when I disobeyed him, going so far as trying to pick me up and carry me there once when I refused to go to therapy. One time when we were alone in the van and he was driving me back from a session, he drove past the turn-off where we lived and onto the highway out of town until there were no longer any streetlights. The dark fields west of the city never looked so remote. He didn't say a word, but I got scared. I felt like he was capable of anything, especially if he'd gone off of his pills. I started to scream at him. I told him to take me home. He turned the van around. I never told my mother.

I knew I would die by my own hand, or maybe my father's, if I stayed there. The next week I told my mother that if she didn't help me move out, I would jump off the overpass by our house. So she did. I moved into my grandmother's house, where eventually I started eating and sleeping again. But this was the start of a terrible time for Karen, because now all of our father's rage was directed at her.

Five months later, though, my mother and siblings joined me. My father had threatened them again and there had been a huge scene when my mother had tried to lock him out of the house, but he had rolled in under the garage door. The police came but they couldn't legally remove him. Karen told me that she was sitting on the roof of the house in the spot where we used to crawl out of the window to hide and that our neighbours were sitting in lawn chairs watching the commotion. Soon after, my parents finally divorced and we got another restraining order against my father. We then moved from my grandmother's house into a duplex one neighbourhood away.

There is still always a chance my father will show up somewhere, but I see him most frequently in my dreams. I have a recurring nightmare that I am still a teenager and that my mother has decided to let my father move back in. When I was younger and had the dream, I would not fight back, but now I will do anything it takes to get rid of him and sometimes I succeed.

Cowboy

MY EARLIEST MEMORY OF the Calgary Stampede involves my parents dressing us up for the parade. I had a whistle and a blue straw cowboy hat with a sheriff's star on the front. My sister had a red one. We were both wearing checkered shirts and Levi's jeans with elastic waistbands. Our brother Craig, a baby at the time, had a bib with a star on it and a brown straw hat that he kept throwing off. Our father was teaching us how to yell "Yee haw!" The rule of the game seemed to be the louder, the better, but every time one of us yelled, it would scare Craig. He would crinkle up his face at first and eventually start to cry. But then that became part of the game. We all took turns yelling "Yee haw" while Craig wailed along.

Every Calgary Stampede, the city becomes a sea of new white cowboy hats and denim worn by office workers who have probably never even been on a farm. You can see them in the evening sauntering around town drunk with little bits of straw stuck on their outfits from the bales of hay that are trucked in for the occasion. I grew up in the suburbs. My father was one of those office workers. I never lived in the country as a child, but my mother's family is different.

I could always tell when my uncle Carl was at my grandma's house when I saw his worn brown cowboy boots at the door. They stood up straight as if his legs were still in them. Uncle Carl lived with his wife and two sons in a mobile home out in the country.

Every once in a while they would decide to move and bring their mobile home with them. I remember being amazed pulling up to the same house in a completely new location. When we walked in everything inside was just the same. It was like a spaceship that could take off and then land somewhere else.

Uncle Carl loved horses. He rode them until he was bow-legged. I would watch him amble around and think about how the horses had changed the shape of his legs to fit their bodies. Sometimes he would take his own horse out for us to ride. He would lift my sister and me up onto it and then lead us around slowly. I felt so tall on top and safe with my uncle holding the reins.

Uncle Carl has worked the oil rigs for as long as I can remember. We would never know if he was going to show up at Christmas or Thanksgiving until that day. It all depended on whether his boss gave the crew the time off or not, and that depended on the price of crude oil. Sometimes he would drive twelve hours straight back from Saskatchewan to be with us. Other times he would be unreachable, working somewhere out on the frozen, flat land. One Christmas when he came home, he hadn't told anyone that he had lost part of a finger a few months earlier, and he made a practical joke out of it. He came up to me and did the trick where he pretended to pull part of his finger off, which is usually done by tucking the finger back and making part of the thumb on the other hand look like it was the detached part of the finger. This time there was no "just kidding" part at the end, and he laughed for half an hour after I screamed when I discovered that there was indeed a part of his finger missing. But I loved it when he paid attention to me even if he sometimes shocked me. I didn't even have any bad feelings for him after he accidentally dislocated my arm when he was trying to put me on his shoulders; I just cried until my relatives gave me candy and then we found out that my arm had popped itself back into its socket on the trip to the emergency room.

My uncles who work the oil rigs are often away from home for months at a time. They work fourteen-hour days or more through every season that the prairies throw at them. All three of them dropped out of high school as soon as they could, but now they earn more money than a lot of people who went to university. Life on the oil rigs is lonely. When I was a child, it was not unusual to get a drunken call from one of my uncles in the middle of the night, wanting to want to talk to all four of us kids to tell us that he loved us. We would make jokes about it and warn each other as we passed the receiver, but I felt my uncles' isolation and identified with it.

When my brother Jack died, they were his pallbearers. They carried his coffin without crying from the church to the hearse. I looked up at them when they passed by me and hoped to be strong like them. When my schizophrenic father would fly off the handle, at least one of them would always show up to protect us. My father was scared of them and would take off as soon as one of them showed up in a truck. They made him look like a tiny guy in a white shirt and thick tie because they were real cowboys. I needed to see that there were people who were unafraid of

Knives and Baseball Bats

ONE DAY WHEN I WAS thirteen, I jumped off the city bus and walked the two blocks home with my trumpet in its case banging against my legs. The thumping sound made the paring knife in my pocket start to feel hot. This knife had been in the kitchen drawer of every house I'd ever lived in. My mother used it to cut apples for us to eat. Fascinated by not being allowed to touch it, I would watch her slice the apples in half and then quarters, then again into eighths. I ate bowls of these apple slices many times a week. Now I had turned the knife against a girl from my softball team. When I arrived home, I walked into the garage and slid it behind the bricks that were piled against the wall.

That spring I had started my second year of softball. I liked the focus of anticipating where the batter might hit the ball, crouching down with my mitt close to the ground. It cleared my mind. I was proud of my blue uniform and felt like a boy in it. The other girls on my team didn't look like boys. Their hairsprayed bangs were crushed down by their hats, but their ponytails hung out the backs and bobbed as they ran from base to base. They would sit on the bench and gossip while I dug my cleats into the red dirt and listened. I would often not speak more than five words during an entire game.

The head coach was a policeman whose daughter was on the team. He wanted her to be a good pitcher, but sometimes she would walk ten people in a row and he'd have to pull her. The parents of the other girls would drive us to games and dot our side of the field with their chairs, cheering loudest for their daughters. Before I would go up to bat, I would try not to look at any of them. My own parents never came to any games. My father was sick and my mother was too busy.

If we won, we would all go to 7-Eleven to get Slurpees before I got dropped back off at my house. My mother would be watching television with my brother John in her arms and my father would still be fast asleep on the couch. By this time, he'd been sleeping most of the days away ever since doctors had put him on another medication in addition to his anti-psychotics, the result of being diagnosed as bipolar. This happened when he was in the hospital and had gone into the stairwell to sing church hymns at the top of his lungs. Even the people in the morgue heard him. When my mother asked him why he had done it, he said that God had sent him a message that He was going to deliver him and he was so overjoyed that he needed to sing.

Some of the girls on my softball team went to my junior high, but they were a year younger. We didn't really talk to each other at school because I had a mushroom haircut, and they were popular and had long hair. I would pass by them in the hall holding my binder to my chest and staring at the ground. I didn't want what they had. I could have styled my hair like theirs and worn the same clothes, but I wanted something that I couldn't name. I had studied these girls, trying to understand them, and I was certain that I wasn't the same.

One of the pitchers was also in concert band with me. Her name was Nadia. She had a surprisingly fast pitch that would thump loudly in the catcher's glove. I liked her more than the other girls on the team because she went out of her way to talk to me. I didn't feel the same cold reserve from her that I felt from the others, especially when my complete lack of pop culture knowledge became obvious, like the time I went to a barbecue and everyone found out that I hadn't seen the video for "Thriller." After the roar of laughter had died down, I spent the rest of the time hanging out on the corner of a couch by myself.

The concert band practiced on Mondays after school once a week, in addition to our regular band classes. Nadia played the clarinet and sat in the row in front of me and my trumpet. For an hour and a half each week, the band would practice stiff-sounding versions of pop songs complete with the squeaks of the first-year saxophone players.

After practice, it took me two city buses to get home. Most of the students took the bus to Brentwood station and then split off according to where they lived. Nadia and some other girls who also lived near me often travelled on the same bus. Most of the time we would have to stand, sometimes for as long as half an hour. Usually I stayed quiet during the ride and listened to the other girls talk. Sometimes Nadia paid attention to me; on those days, I could feel my face glow as I walked home.

And then one time on the way home, one of the other girls made a comment about how I looked like a boy, and Nadia looked at me and laughed. I felt a darkness rise within me. *I'll show them*, I thought. *They won't be laughing next time.*

I carried that anger with me over the weekend until Monday, the next time we had concert band practice. That morning I went to the kitchen before anyone in my house was awake, got the paring knife from the drawer, and shoved it into the bottom of my backpack. All day long at school, I was nervous about it being there. I spent more time thinking about getting caught with it than what my plans for it were.

After practice, I caught the same bus as Nadia and the other girls to Brentwood station. I didn't say a word to any of them. When we were at the bus stop at Brentwood, one of the girls started in on me again. It was then that I pulled the knife out of my backpack and waved it at Nadia coldly. "You better fuck off," I growled between my teeth.

There was a look of shock on her face before she turned to run. I watched her and the other girls bolt up the stairs and across the overpass. When my bus came, I stashed the knife and got aboard. That night, I tried my best to keep quiet about what happened as we ate dinner.

The next morning I didn't see Nadia or any of the girls from the bus stop. I went to first period without incident, but during second period science class, the intercom rang on the wall. "They want you in the office," the teacher said to me. As I walked down the empty hall toward the principal's office, I could feel prickling on the back of my neck. The secretary took my name and I sat down and waited. Soon, the principal called me into his office. "Nadia's mom called this morning and told us that you chased her and some other girls with a knife," he said. "I should expel you. Now, there are only two reasons why you would do that. Either you're a bad kid or you're a sick kid."

I had never been in trouble like this before. I thought fast. If I was a bad kid, I would be expelled. If I was a sick kid, they would send me to the hospital. I broke down crying, unsure if I was faking it.

"I'm not a bad kid," I wailed. "I didn't mean to do it. I wasn't going to hurt them."

The principal then sent me to see the guidance counselor, who took a softer tone with me.

"Why did you do it?" he asked.

I told him why I had chased them, that I just wanted to scare them, and where I had hidden the knife. I told him about how my dad was sick and how he kept going off of his pills and yelling at me. When I said that I wanted to kill myself, he seemed to understand what I needed.

"I think you might need to go to the hospital for a while," he said.

"Can I take my guitar?" I asked.

"Of course," he said gently. I felt relieved.

He told me to go wait in another room. As I sat there under the fluorescent lights, I pictured myself in a hospital room away from my family. At least then I wouldn't have to worry about my father trying to take us all away again.

I heard a knock at the door. It was my parents. My heart immediately started racing. *What are they doing there? I told him I needed to get away from them.* The counselor followed them into the room and said, "I've spoken to your parents and we feel that it's best if you go home with them. They've assured me that your father is getting treatment and doing much better. You need to understand that he was sick, but he's recovered now. The best place for you to learn that is with your family."

In the car, we rode home in silence. I looked for the knife in the garage, but it was gone. It seemed from then on, the narrative of our family suddenly changed. I had done something to confirm that I was messed up. It wasn't all in my father's head.

The next day, news about what I did went around the school. Students alternately stared or grinned at me in the hall. One girl came up to me and called me "Little knifer girl," which became my nickname for the rest of junior high. It was meant to make me feel bad, but actually it made me feel tougher. *Maybe I am a bad kid*, I thought. At least then others would think twice about making fun of me.

Bible Camp

MY MOTHER USED TO tell me stories about swimming in the lakes near Bowden, Alberta where she grew up. They were a bit deeper than the sloughs we splashed through in boots on my Uncle Carl's property, but not too different. My mother would say, "After swimming we would emerge from the water with leeches on our legs, but that never discouraged us. We would just put salt on the leeches, or Uncle Carl would hold a match to them until they fell off."

As for me, I've hated water since my father threw me into a pool to teach me how to swim when I was four. I would make an exception for the clear waters of Okanagan lakes, but murky prairie ones were out of the question.

When I was fourteen, during the summer between junior and senior high, my parents drove me out to Spruce Lake to spend a week at Bible camp. Spruce Lake was very close to Bowden. Pressing my face against the car window during the drive into camp, I was certain it would turn out to be one of the fabled lakes of torment from my mother's stories.

At camp, I stayed in the girls' dorm. I had an easier time with Christian girls than non-Christian ones. They had to be nice to me, even if I looked like a boy, because we were sisters in Christ. My hair was long, black, and parted in the middle. It hung in front of my eyes. I looked like an escapee from a grunge video compared to all of the proper Christian girls in their oversized T-shirts and denim shorts. I couldn't bring myself to giggle with them about things like makeup or boys. As a result, I couldn't manage to make friends with any of them. I felt like I was a dark cloud hovering in my bunk bed above them.

I was never baptized because of my combined fear of speaking in front of crowds and being submerged in water. When the entire camp went swimming in the lake for the afternoon, I refused to go. As the upbeat masses of teens thinned out and eventually disappeared, I could see that there was one other camper who felt the same way as I did: a boy with stringy bleached hair who was playing a guitar on the deck outside of the cafeteria. I wondered why I hadn't noticed him earlier. I went back to my room and dragged my guitar in its heavy case across the camp.

We spent the afternoon together sitting on the patio of the mess hall exchanging Nirvana covers. Between songs he told me that he was from Edmonton and that his father had taught him how to busk on Whyte Avenue. He made Edmonton sound way better than Calgary. I envied his freedom and pictured myself singing to crowds of people in the street while they threw quarters into my guitar case. "What are you doing here, then?" I asked. "Shouldn't you be back there making money?"

"My dad didn't have time to watch me and I kept getting in trouble, so he sent me here," he replied.

"So, you're not a Christian?" I blurted out.

"Nah. These people are crazy. I wish I could go home to my electric guitar. Are you?"

Forgetting to impress him, I told him the truth. "I don't know."

The other teens returned from the lake that afternoon, sunburned and exhausted. Dinner in the cafeteria got really quiet when they all bowed their heads and one of the camp leaders prayed over the meal. I stared at the black nail polish I had chipped off my fingers while I played guitar. I was thinking about the boy who didn't believe in any of this.

Every night we had a service in the main chapel attended by the entire camp. On that particular night, the air outside still felt warm. The setting sun was hanging low in the sky as we filed in. The inside of the church looked more like a cabin. Huge wooden beams held up the roof and anchored the walls. There was a screen on the stage where the lyrics of songs were displayed with an overhead projector. The night began with a sermon by the camp pastor about how faith was the only thing separating humans from hell. I slouched low in the pew with my hands in my pockets. It felt like the words were directed right at me. I was desperate to recover from my uncertainty. I wanted to believe. It was the only option I was being given. At the end of the sermon, the camp pastor made a plea for anyone who needed help from Jesus to come to the front. I rose and nervously made my way up. With each step I begged that God would give me a sign. I joined a small group at the front as everyone started praying. Lifting my hands up, I concentrated as hard as I could: *One sign and I'll believe in you forever, I swear*, I whispered.

The boy standing next to me started to speak in tongues.

"Shaklaka lakkwakateeheeoh."

The pastor heard him and came over to where he was standing. He put his hand on the boy's forehead and started to pray out loud: "Lord Jesus, you have brought this young man before us to speak your holy language. Let the holy spirit bring him peace as he obeys your will." The boy swayed back and forth violently and then shot backwards, falling toward the floor. The people behind him caught him and lowered him gently. I looked at him out of the corner of my half-closed eye. He was laying on his back with a serene look on his face and tears rolling down his cheeks.

I had never spoken in tongues, which I took to be another sign that I was not willing enough to be faithful. I felt intensely jealous of the boy on the floor. I want to be chosen by Jesus. The pastor then moved on to me. I prayed hard as he put his hand on my forehead. "Sweet Lord. We have a girl here who needs your help to be faithful. Please show your presence in this room and reveal to her your limitless love. Amen." I was waiting for a feeling, but before anything happened I felt the pastor's hand push hard against my head. I fell backwards and people caught me. "Praise Jesus," he said and moved on to the next person.

I lay on my back on the floor, numb, my eyes closed. I was certain that it was the pastor who had pushed me. I hadn't even the tiniest sense of God being in the room. I decided to just lay there rather than stand up, lest he push me back down again. I stayed in that position for what felt like forever. When I finally opened my eyes, there were other people laying on the floor and everyone else had formed a conga line that was making its way around the church. I realized then that even if there was a God, He wasn't going to speak to or through me.

At the end of the week, my parents picked me up. As we drove home, I stared at the rows of trees that farmers had planted to keep the wind from blowing the soil on their land around.

"They're always the same height," I said, pointing them out to my mother.

"Uncle Carl used to tell me that they're like that because the farmers would trim them with an upside down helicopter," she said, chuckling. "For a long time, because he was my hero, I believed him."

Hide and Seek

WHEN I WAS A CHILD, the eight-hour drive through the Rocky Mountains to British Columbia seemed like it took a week. The mountains always started out high and grey. I would put my head back and imagine that they were sleeping giants, and I would look for upturned faces and resting limbs in the rocks. High waterfalls would spray tears out of the giants' hidden eyes. After the summit they would disintegrate into the low scrubby mountains of the Okanagan, and then I would know that we were close to my grandparents' house.

Once there, I would often turn my mind to the cherry tree that grew in the yard of my grandparents' neighbours. Its branches hung down low enough that we could reach them and pick our own fruit. At home I would try the crabapples from our tree, but when I bit them in half I had to spit them out onto our lawn; they were too sour to eat. But the cherries were delicious. We would fill our hats with them, staining our faces and hands purple when we ate them.

One time after we arrived following the long drive, I was eager to show our grandfather that I knew how to turn a TV on. I was so caught up in my excitement that I didn't hear him yell at me as I ran toward it: "Don't touch my TV!"

I pulled the knob, but as soon as the signal clicked on I felt myself being lifted up into the air. He shook me and yelled in my face. "I told you not to touch my TV!"

The next time we went back to visit, it was because our grandfather was in the hospital with lung cancer. I'd never seen him smoke, but he did until he was too sick to go outside. On this visit he couldn't even raise his head to acknowledge us, a ventilator pumping oxygen into his failing lungs. He was now weaker than I was.

Our grandfather started working on the railroad in Saskatchewan when he was sixteen. Our father grew up with his four brothers and sisters in an old railway station outside of Regina. He described the rumble of the trains as they passed right by his house. At night, he said, he would lay on the floor of his room and listen through the vents to the radio playing downstairs. He told us about the boredom and how he would put pieces of metal on the tracks so the trains would crush them. All of his siblings ran away as soon as they could to make lives elsewhere, but he was the youngest and ended up in Penticton after his parents retired there. Our father was obsessed with train sets and would show me tiny versions of pulley trains my grandfather had ridden, propelling them with his arms.

Our grandmother had to be strong in order to live as long as she did with a cruel man like our grandfather. She used to work cleaning motel rooms, and our father told me she'd come home aching from twelve-hour shifts and then have to cook dinner. I remember her only when she was much older, a tiny woman with white hair and bright, playful blue eyes. I gravitated toward her because she paid attention to me, reading to me for hours, drawing pictures for me, and telling me stories about her father being late for the boat from England to Australia: "And that's why we live in Canada. Because he missed the boat!" she'd say, laughing.

When she was twelve, her parents sent her to live at her uncle's farm. She spent her days in the fields picking weeds. "It was hard work and I was very young," she told me once. "I never figured out why they sent me away."

I didn't discover until I was a teenager that our grandmother met our grandfather because she was caring for his kids. His first wife had been institutionalized and my grandmother had been hired as a nanny. Within a year, she was pregnant. He sent the children from his first marriage away to their mother's parents and married my grandmother.

When I learned how to write, I sent letters to her, and she would write me back. I once sent her a letter in code and she took the time to decipher it and reply. She liked collecting pencils, spoons, and things with birds on them. She loved birds and had two of them; one of them was a canary named Mikey.

After my grandfather died and she started to forget things like the stove being on, her children decided that it was time to sell the house. By then she'd become very anxious, probably because she could sense that control was slowly being taken away from her. They told her it was for the best, and when the house was sold they each took a portion of the proceeds from the sale. Then they took turns passing her around between them until one day she and her canary came to live at our house. A big moving van arrived from the Okanagan, and soon a quarter of our basement was filled with piles of her boxes and furniture. "She wanted to bring it all with her," my uncle explained.

"But she won't need it here," my father said.

"I tried to tell her. You know how she's getting … " my uncle snorted.

I was excited about my grandma moving in with us. My mother had recently given birth to my brother John and my father ignored me for the most part; he had insomnia so he slept a lot during the day, and the rest of the time he was at work. But my grandmother had changed. She couldn't read well or draw anymore and she would often accuse us of stealing her watch or other things that she'd misplaced. She would sit for hours in the only chair that my father let her use from her belongings in the basement. I wanted to make her happy, but I didn't know how.

One Sunday night, my father was in a rare good mood and decided that we should all play hide and seek. As he started to count, we all ran to hide. One by one he found all of us except my grandmother. The whole family went through the house calling out to her. Soon we heard laughing coming from the family room, but when we got there we couldn't see her. I crawled on my knees and looked under the coffee table and then in a space between her armchair and the wall. There I found her, crouched down with a huge smile on her face, her blue eyes shining brightly, her finger to her lips.

Mikey the canary died a few weeks after that. I found him at the bottom of his cage. When I showed my grandmother, she didn't seem upset. She just stared blankly at the bird and went back to her chair. Meanwhile, my father's behaviour was becoming increasingly erratic, so my mother asked my aunt in Penticton to take my grandmother. After she moved, I wanted to write her letters, but I knew she couldn't read anymore.

By the time I saw her again she could barely put a sentence together. She kept trying to run away from my aunt's house, but she couldn't figure out how to open the inside lock on the doors. She would buzz around from room to room muttering to herself; other times she would refuse to get out of bed all day. They decided it was time to put her in a nursing home. The last time I saw her she was lying in a bed in a darkened room, and we got to eat ice cream with her. She pulled her head up to eat some off the spoon that the nurse offered her. All of us sat in chairs eating ours in silence, because she didn't seem to understand us when we spoke. All of the things I had loved about her and all of her memories of me were gone.

When she died, we didn't go to the funeral, and I don't remember crying. It had been such a long time coming. Much later, my cousin told me a story I hadn't heard before: one afternoon, my grandmother managed to break out of the nursing home. To leave the yard, all you had to do was punch a password into a panel and the locked gates would open. My grandmother couldn't do that, so she pushed a lawn chair up to the fence and climbed over. My cousin went to look for her and found her eating candy in a corner store. "I bought her the candy and drove her back to the home and they kept a closer eye on her there after that," he said, shrugging. My heart jumped. *So she had tried to break free.* She knew what she was doing, at least until she got out. I could picture her smiling to herself on the other side of the fence, her blue eyes twinkling, just before she forgot where she was again.

Healing Meeting

THERE'S A SEA SNAKE that's rumoured to live in the Okanagan Valley, where my father's family lived. On the annual drive there from Calgary, the four of us kids would spread out in our two-tone brown Ford van, sweating on the vinyl bench seats as we crossed through the mountains. Our bare legs would get burnt on the hot seatbelt buckles. Pro-life signs dotted the sides of the picturesque mountains and lakes, punctuated by the odd fruit stand.

The waters of Okanagan Lake, stretching from Penticton to Vernon, are the deepest blue. The sea snake purported to be living there is named Ogopogo, after a 1920s dancehall song, but it's known in Salish as Naitaka (Lake Demon). My cousin Ben told me that scientists have never found the bottom of the lake because it's on an angle that goes under one of the cities; I imagined that this was where the sea snake slept: under my uncle's house, curled up at night, not too far below us. Whenever my cousins and I waded more than a hundred metres out into the water, the creature suddenly became a horror film monster. Someone would always yell "Ogopogo!" and all eight of us would rush clumsily through the deep water until we were back on shore, panting but safe. We would return to our beach towels, but when we got too hot, we would venture back into the water until someone called out "Ogopogo" again, sending us into another fit of panic.

Some summers later, the signs of danger became more personal.

By then my father had spent a few years in and out of the mental health institutions in Calgary. I was slowly figuring out that despite the fact that he was struggling with paranoia, he was also wholly abusive. He could see his control over me starting to slip, and that made him want to assert himself even more.

One August I was sitting in my aunt's living room in Penticton, wishing that we could go back to Calgary where I had left my roller blades, when she rushed into the kitchen. My parents were sitting at the table. I was laying low on the couch so they wouldn't notice me through the gap between the living room and the kitchen.

My aunt began to talk excitedly. "I just went to a tent meeting near the church. There was a pastor there from Texas. Remember how one of my legs has always been shorter than the other?"

When they were children, Aunty Cindy had fallen down the stairs while holding my father. The leg she broke in the fall ended up an inch shorter than the other. "Well, there was a prayer service after and I went up to the front. He was praying over me and asked if I wanted to be healed. I told him about my leg and he touched my head. I fell backwards and when I stood up, it was an inch longer!" I curled up on the couch, wondering snidely why she hadn't chosen to heal her husband, whose legs had been partially amputated because of a logging truck accident. It seemed off to me, but my parents were hungry Pentecostals and always looking for some kind of spiritual revival. They decided that our whole family would go visit the pastor from Texas. The next morning we piled into our van, with my aunt and uncle behind us in theirs, and we all headed off for the tent on the side of the highway, which turned out to be a plain white vinyl dome filled with rows of folding chairs. We sat near the back with my uncle Andrew on the aisle as the tent began to fill up. A half hour later a man walked across the front to a tiny wooden pulpit. He was wearing a grey suit with brown cowboy boots and a white Stetson hat. He said to the congregation that he had come all the way to Canada because God had told him to come north to heal people. I saw that my aunt's eyes were gleaming as he explained this.

He then spoke for about an hour on the subject of being saved. When I was much younger I had made the choice about where I was going to spend eternal life, so I allowed my mind to wander. I pictured him taking off his hat and passing it around instead of an offering plate, and then putting it back onto his head full of money and walking out.

He started singing as a sheet of paper was passed around for people to sign up who wanted to be healed. Out of boredom, I leaned over to my parents and said rebelliously, "I should get my eyes healed. I'm tired of wearing glasses." When the sheet of paper got to us, I saw my father scribble something on it, but assumed he was just looking for another opportunity to speak in tongues in front of a crowd.

Someone began reading the names out one by one, and those whose names were called would walk up to the front of the congregation. The pastor from Texas would then approach them and ask if they wanted to be healed. He would talk about faith and how Jesus wanted them to have it. I heard my name called, and then my father's. Stunned, I stood up and walked to the front, my father right behind me. I knew if I bolted, I would be grounded for months. I decided that the best thing to do was to go along with it. The pastor from Texas asked me what I needed healed. "My eyes," I mumbled into his dented microphone. And then he prayed for me, repeating that only those with faith would be healed. I rolled my eyes under their closed lids. It would be over soon. I wasn't going to speak in gibberish or fall backwards. I wasn't even sure there was a God.

Next it was my father's turn. He told the pastor from Texas that he wanted to be healed from his sleep apnea. My father put on a better show than me, getting worked up over his healing and even shedding a small tear or two. We then sat down and everyone put as much money in the offering plate as I had imagined being in his hat.

Our vacation was over the next day. We made the eight-hour drive home without once mentioning what had happened. I took off my glasses and squinted at the mountains a bunch of times before putting them back on, wondering if I could be healed when I didn't believe.

Back in Calgary, the regular power struggles between my father and me resumed. There was an ongoing fight over whose version of reality was correct. He told us that we were making him sick, which I thought was unfair. He thought that I should believe him when he said that he had received an e-mail from God. One of the fights got so heated that I brought up his hospitalization as proof of my point. He said, "Yes. I was sick, but God healed me of everything at that tent meeting in Penticton."

I was fifteen. I lost my place in the argument. I could have thrown my glasses at him or brought up the fact that his snoring the night before had reminded me of an enraged bear, but I was trapped. My attacks had to be strategic. They had to be just enough to make me feel like I was surviving, but not push him to violence. I never measured my aunt's leg or even looked at it to see if she was telling the truth. The truth doesn't matter in survival situations. So I took the most alive parts of myself and hid them deep under our house, like a sea snake trying to stay out of view.

Respect the Wheel

WHEN I WAS FIFTEEN, I moved to my maternal grandmother's house in the northeast section of Calgary. My fights with my father had intensified to dangerous levels. He had decided that I had been doing drugs, so he invited a cop who was a family friend to come over and talk to me about it. I hadn't done many drugs, at least no more than anyone else at school. I was angry after the family friend left. I trashed my entire room and threatened to jump off the overpass near our house if I had to stay there any longer. I wasn't bluffing, and I think my mother could tell. I packed all of my belongings into the back of our car, and I didn't use boxes. I just ran back and forth from my room to the car with my arms full of stuff. It was piled so high, you couldn't see through the rear view mirror. My father was against the move, but my mother stood up to him on my behalf. Ironically, they drove me to my grandmother's house together. When we arrived, I moved my things in by the same method, carrying them in my arms and piling them on the floor of the basement room with two-tone blue shag carpeting and wallpaper from the 1950s.

My Uncle Jim lived with my grandmother for as long as I can remember. He left home when he was sixteen to go logging, but moved back in with her months later when a tree fell on him and broke his spinal cord. As kids we used to ride his wheelchair lift up and down on the porch for fun, and he let us do wheelies in his spare chair in the basement. Uncle Jim called me "Homer" because when he and my grandmother came to one of my softball games, I had hit my only two home runs, crying with joy the first time while I rounded the bases. My uncle snuck me a twenty-dollar bill after the game, which seemed like a small fortune at the time.

On my first day at Grandma's, Uncle Jim told me that there really was only one important rule in the house: "Respect the Wheel." This meant that I had to be home for *Wheel of Fortune*, which was on every night at eight-thirty. There was an elaborate ritual. First, each of us had to pick one of the contestants to root for. There were always three of them and three of us, so it worked out perfectly. We selected them by calling numbers during the opening of the show before we got to see them. If our contestant won, then we won. We could also win by solving the puzzles. My grandmother was very good at it, but she would often lose because she would sound the puzzles out loud, which usually gave us a clue to the solution. That was only if we were watching it together, though; there was a television in every room of the house except the bathroom, and sometimes we would all watch in our separate rooms, screaming the answers to each other across the house. Uncle Jim was in love with Vanna White. We pretended she was his girlfriend. "All of these years and she looks so good," he would say.

One night my uncle decided to play a practical joke on us and watched an earlier broadcast of the show on a different channel at six. He started the game by modestly getting the answers right, but when he got the right answer before any letters were on the board, my grandmother and I started to wonder. We laughed until we were out of breath when he admitted his secret. We didn't mind he'd broken the only rule.

After a few weeks of the Wheel, I started to feel better about myself. My grandmother and I would wake up at five in the morning and she'd watch the Weather Channel with me before my hour-and-a-half commute to high school. She sent me to school with lunches of bologna sandwiches, chocolate bars, and apples. For dinner she would make all of my favourite foods, and I would try to eat everything she put on my plate. I started sleeping again, too. I got to take one sleeping pill a night, and I didn't have to listen to my father's nightly rants anymore. I also stopped going to church; my grandmother asked me once if I wanted to go and I said no. She never asked again or bothered me about it. There was a feeling of togetherness in her house. My uncle and I would gang up on my grandmother and tease her, singing loud Christmas carols out of tune during the holidays. She said that she hated it, but I saw in her eyes that she didn't really.

At my grandmother's house I learned that I was not a bad kid. I was actually really good at following the rules. I took the chores they assigned me seriously. I would shovel all the snow off the sidewalks around the house, chip the ice off with a pick, and then sweep away any remaining snow with a broom. I didn't want my grandmother or my uncle to slip on the ice, which gave both of them so much trouble in the winter.

My grandmother accepted me far more than my parents ever

did. She'd never liked my father. We shared the same opinion: he was a tyrant. She spent her entire life taking care of her family, raising six children alone after my grandfather, who was the pastor of a church in small town, ran off with one of the elementary school teachers. My grandmother put a lien on his church and got the piano to make up for unpaid child support at a time when there was no protection for women whose husbands had left them. She always beats me in Scrabble and can play the piano, organ, and accordion by ear, and even made herself a steel guitar by playing a regular acoustic with a butter knife. Never critical of me for not being feminine enough when I was a child and loving sports, she watches every Toronto Blue Jays game she can on TV. But my grandmother is also a Baptist and holds a lot of conservative opinions. Even though my first kiss took place in my tiny room in her basement, I have never told her that I am queer or trans. She has said a lot of homophobic things and I know she would not appreciate the revelation or bend her rules to accept me. Jesus was the only thing that got her through all of those years. Without Him, she would have had no one on her side. So I respect the silence about certain things between us, and she never ventures to expose the truth.

We are from different eras, but my grandmother and I have more similarities than our love of sports and music. When we were putting together a slide show for her seventy-fifth birthday, my sister found a tiny photo in a box and e-mailed it to me. It was of a woman in a wedding dress and a man in a suit. I was confused because I didn't think the woman looked like my grandmother, but then I noticed that the man looked a lot like me. It was her, smiling with her arm through the other woman's, dressed in drag sometime in the 1940s. When my sister asked her about it, she said, "Oh, that was silly. I don't know why we did that." I guess we are both keeping secrets from each other.

Outsiders

I MET RENA BECAUSE our last names were near each other in the alphabet. We were seated alphabetically in school, and no one in our Career and Life Management class had a last name starting with the letter between ours. I was sixteen and she had just turned seventeen. That first day I spent the entire class looking straight ahead. When I turned around, I noticed how beautiful she was. I wanted to talk to her, but didn't know what to say. So I said, "Your purse looks like a dead rat." To my surprise, she laughed. The next day I grabbed her eraser and sawed it in half with my pencil in a second awkward gesture of friendship. She didn't seem to mind, and soon we became allies in making fun of our teacher, especially when he tried to instill in us the value of investing in mutual funds and real estate. We were teenagers, after all; I was more worried about if I'd get away with skipping a class or who was going to buy my cigarettes.

We had to pair up to work on a project about current social issues, so Rena and I decided to work together. When the topics were pulled out of a hat, we got schizophrenia. *At least I know a lot about it*, I thought.

The weekend we were supposed to put together our project, my father was hospitalized for threatening my family. I met up with Rena at the public library. Although we hadn't been friends for long, she could tell something was off. "What's going on with you today?" she asked. "You're really quiet."

"I don't feel well," I mumbled.

"Come on. You don't seem sick. Did something happen?" she prodded.

I had been hiding my father's episodes since they began, but Rena's eyes were kind, and gazing into them made me want to tell her the truth. "My dad is a schizophrenic," I whispered. "I found out when I was eleven. Every once in a while, he flips out and ends up in the hospital. Yesterday, it happened again."

"Why didn't you tell me that before?" she asked. "We could have switched or something."

"I didn't want to make a big deal about it," I said. "But reading about schizophrenia is really making me feel bad."

"Listen, I'll do the research and write the text," she said. "How about you just draw and colour the pictures of the brains for our poster?"

So we sat there together in the library all afternoon, Rena taking notes while I coloured in pictures beside her. Occasionally, I would steal a look at her leaning over the books with her hair hanging in her face.

On Monday when we made our class presentation, I was so out of it I could barely speak. I had gotten a call from my mother that morning and found out that she had planned to let my father come home after he got out the hospital. Even though I didn't live with them anymore, I was really tired of the same thing happening over and over. I just stood next to Rena as I held up the red poster board with little pictures and bits of text glued to it, staring at the floor. When we sat down, the teacher said, "This is a great project, Rena, but Rae doesn't seem to know much about it."

I didn't bother arguing. The weekend I had just been through wasn't something I felt like explaining as part of the project. Besides, Rena was in the advanced program and I had basically given up on school altogether. I'd barely passed any of my courses—even music, where I had neglected theory to write songs.

"Don't worry about it," Rena said after class, touching my shoulder before walking away. My eyes followed her down the hallway.

Since Rena knew about my father, I stopped hiding things from her. We started passing notes to each other in class and then ones we had written between classes. Through these notes, we learned each other's secrets. Rena loaned me her favourite book, *The Outsider* by Albert Camus. I devoured every page of it. She also introduced me to the Smiths. I would walk around the suburbs with them reverberating in the headphones of a yellow Walkman that she loaned me. Soon, all I thought about was Rena. I rehashed our conversations when we were apart and glowed when we were together.

Then Rena wrote in a note that she wanted me to see her favourite movie, *Heathers*. I wrote back and invited her to stay over and watch the movie. That Friday we took the bus back to my grandma's house. I talked nervously during the entire ride. I had a warm tickle in my stomach that wouldn't go away. I hoped Rena couldn't tell. A few months earlier I had come out as gay to a friend whom

I'd had many sleepovers with and she had told me that she wanted to stop being friends. I didn't want that to happen again.

At dinner, my grandmother tried to feed Rena roast beef, even though she had announced she was a vegetarian. I don't think I had ever met one before, so I was as confused as my grandma when Rena refused it. We fed her broccoli and mashed potatoes instead. Then we watched her videotape of *Heathers* in the living room, sitting close to each other on the couch. When it was time to go to bed, we said goodnight to my grandmother and headed to my room in the basement of the house. I went to the bathroom and changed into my pajamas and then Rena did the same. We stayed up talking quietly until the sky turned from black to dark blue and the birds started singing.

We began sleeping at each other's houses every weekend. Eventually, hiding my sexuality started to feel deceitful, considering I had told her all of my other secrets. One day, I decided to tell her.

Sitting cross-legged facing one another on her bed on a Friday afternoon, I told her I had something to tell her, but then I stumbled on my words. "Write it down," she said, and passed a piece of paper to me.

I picked up an orange marker and wrote "I am gay," then folded up the note and passed it back to her. She unfolded it and read it. The back of my neck grew hot with the looming possibility of being abandoned again. But then she raised her head and said, "I'm not homophobic." A wave of relief washed over me. I wasn't going to lose her. We then decided to rip up the note and burn it in the backyard. We knew how dangerous those words were if left lying around. Life went back to normal; we kept passing notes and sleeping at each other's houses. A few months later, I knew I couldn't hide my other secret either. I liked her. I'd always liked her.

On one of the last days of school that June, I shakily wrote out another note. Actually, it was more like a survey. In it, I put two questions.

The first was: "Do you think you could date a girl?"

The second read: "Do you think you could like me?"

Next to each question, I put two boxes for her to check: one said "Yes" and the other said "No." At the end of lunchtime, I handed the note to her, then went to my afternoon classes. I knew I was gambling with our friendship and all of my happiness. When she handed it back after school, I opened it cautiously. Inside she had checked the "Yes" box for both questions. I felt like the prairie wind was lifting me right off of the ground.

That night, she came to sleep over at my grandmother's house again. We lay across from each other on top of the blankets. Neither of us had ever kissed anyone before. It occurred to me that I didn't know how. We spent a lot of time listening to a Simon and Garfunkel record and awkwardly figuring out how to match the feelings we had with our bodies. It was somehow perfect because it was much safer than I had ever felt having anyone so close to me.

Then it came an abrupt halt. Rena went to England to visit her family for seven weeks. The day after she left, I had my first panic attack. I was alone in my room when it occurred to me that she could die before I ever saw her again. I couldn't talk to anyone about it, and in my paranoid state it grew into the thought that she probably *would* die before I ever saw her again. I had someone I wanted more than anything. Given my history, it seemed logical that she would be taken away. My love turned into a quiet desperation. I did everything I could to distract myself. There were no letters and no phone calls, no proof that she was alive beside the fact that no one had called me to tell me otherwise. But then, maybe her family wouldn't call me even if something did happen.

When Rena finally came home, I didn't recognize her at first. I felt like I was looking up out of the bottom of a well. She had been in London and Amsterdam, where she shopped and even went to a Michael Jackson concert. She was wearing makeup and different earrings. She said she had written, but her letters would take six weeks to arrive. She felt like she couldn't call because her family was nosy and she wasn't sure if they would have eavesdropped. I couldn't put into words the terror of my daily panic attacks. It took a week for things to start to feel the same as they did before she left.

The first day of grade twelve, I found out what it was like to try to hide something that I was very excited about. I would see Rena between classes and want to grab her hand or kiss her. By lunch hour it became unbearable, and we stole away to an alley near the school, so we could be close for a minute.

"This is really hard," I said. "Whenever I see you, I want to kiss you."

"I know," she replied. "It's really messed up that we have to hide something I feel so good about."

That was also the year that Ellen came out on national TV. We watched the show together with the volume on low in my basement room. Now we knew that there were places we could run to where being queer was okay, like San Francisco or Los Angeles. Rena and I became bolder. We started to tell our friends that we were together. After it became clear that most people at high school already knew, we gave up and started to do whatever we wanted even though we had to endure people hurling insults at us constantly.

One day a friend at school said to me, "Hey Rae, I hear you've got rights." I didn't know what she was talking about, but she explained that a teacher had won a discrimination case filed with the Alberta Human Rights Commission after he was fired from a Christian school for being gay, which led to sexual orientation being protected under provincial human rights legislation. All day I walked around the school chanting, "You can't hurt me, I have rights," at all the other students. One girl came up to me and said, "I don't believe in you."

"I don't care if you believe in me," I said. "Just don't beat me up."

I thought that Rena and I were going to get married. That's what people who were in love were supposed to do. We just had to make it through the last year of high school. We talked about having children together and what we might name them. We were totally absorbed in the way that people can be when they've never broken up before. It was supposed to last forever.

But we were both extremely jealous and would sometimes fight terribly. There was so much outside pressure that when we finally did graduate from high school, our relationship fell apart. Rena went to university and I got a job at a gas station. Graduation was not the finish line, but it was the beginning of our separate lives.

Our affair is over now, but it still exists in the memories of all of the nights we spent together talking and listening to old records in my basement as teenagers. I can go back to those moments and remember how complete I felt. She was the first person that I ever felt safe to be myself around. It gave me hope that I could construct something secure and new for myself. It gave me a reason to work out the ugliness inside me. I spent the next ten years wrestling with my past, but Rena was always somewhere nearby to remind me why it was worth the fight.

Drunk in the Spirit

IN MY EARLY TEENAGE years, I went to church events five times a week, and our parents hosted a Bible study at our house every Wednesday. My father wanted to boost his reputation around town in case people found out about him being hospitalized for a paranoid breakdown. It seemed important to him that church members saw him sitting there at home, in a circle of chairs with a Bible in his lap, while my mother served coffee and we, his children, sat silently nearby. We mostly obeyed except for an early incident when we carefully lowered a purple slinky from the stairs above onto the pastor's head. It was a rare moment of slapstick in the midst of our family's display of "normality," and fortunately comedic enough that we weren't punished. Wednesday nights were boring, but at least we were allowed to drink coffee.

On Friday nights my sister and I were sent off to the church youth group, where hot pizzas, fake graffiti, and loud Christian rap were used to show us the cool side of Jesus: Jesus the skateboarder. Jesus our buddy. Jesus with a flying V guitar. Our youth group had a pool table and its own yellow school bus that would whisk us off to bowling alleys or even larger gatherings of faithful teens. The church also organized youth-oriented sermons designed to keep us from turning into sinners as adults. One Friday an expert on homosexuality preached to us about the perils of "Adam and Steve." He never mentioned how he became such an expert on gayness, but his talk affected me a lot. I left feeling like a solid sheet of ice had formed over my sexuality. Not only was I certain that I wasn't gay, I was also certain that I wasn't straight. I believed I was above sex altogether. It was convenient for me that the next guest speaker was from an abstinence organization. After illustrating the vulnerability of the unmarried to all STIs, the horrors of teen pregnancy, and the consequences of eternal damnation, he handed out pink cards for us to sign that read: "Father God, in the Name of Jesus, this day I commit to glorifying you with my body, soul, and spirit. I offer my body as a living sacrifice, and I pledge to commit to abstinence until marriage, which is my reasonable service. I recognize that at times I may feel tempted or weak, but it's in these times that I will seek strength and guidance from You and Your Word. I can do nothing in and of myself, however I can do all things through Christ who strengthens me, including henceforth abstaining from sex until marriage. In Jesus's Name, Amen."

That speaker was careful to tell us that those who agreed to sign would be brought up to the front of the church on Sunday morning to celebrate their commitment to abstinence with the entire congregation. Of course, this meant that anyone who didn't sign would be left to sit in their seats under the disapproving eye of other churchgoers. The open refusal of abstinence would be social suicide; it would mean being banned from activities outside of church and shamed from within it. Every single person at youth group signed their card that night, and on the following Sunday, we all marched proudly up to the front of the church. I don't know

that the bad things that had happened to my family were all part of God's plan. She may have had more than a spiritual interest in me. I will never know, though, because I assume she followed the pledge on her pink card right into holy matrimony with a good Christian man.

On Saturday nights my church had a more casual sermon in the main room. The band would break out the electric pianos, synthesizers, and electric guitars for praise and worship. We would wear dress pants and sweater vests. The more casual the dress code, the more Pentecostal the expressions of the church members would be. It was almost like a youth service for all ages, with everyone from children to people in their eighties praising fervently. Between songs, the band would keep quietly repeating chords while the pastor made rambling, improvised speeches beseeching us to come to God. By attending the service, I thought we had technically done our bit to go to Him, but there were other ways to get even closer to the Lord, including speaking in tongues and being slain in the spirit. The most confusing of the possibilities to me was what my mother called being drunk in the spirit, a kind of all-of-the-above option which involved both falling over and speaking in tongues. It was odd to me that it had that name because no one in the congregation was allowed to drink—alcohol was far too destructive to our bodies, which were temples for the Lord. It was the only way we were allowed to "get drunk." Mostly it was a way for churchgoers to blow off steam on the weekend after working office jobs for oil companies all week, a generous concession from God because he seemed to understand how stressful life in Calgary could be for sober people.

The traditional service took place on Sunday mornings. The pastor's wife alternately played the piano and the organ. We sang from the hymn books in the pews in front of us. I hated the music but loved to follow the notes and in doing so learned to harmonize out of boredom. I felt awkward in my Sunday clothes, which usually meant a dress, a skirt, or a pair of skorts. I felt like a cat in a T-shirt, but at least when I was singing my voice could blend in, and I felt that I belonged. The sermons were long and seemed to get more urgent when coupled with the intense hunger that would build inside me. No matter how much cereal I ate for breakfast, I always felt like I was going to pass out from hunger at least half an hour before the sermon ended. Sunday mornings were a true test of faith.

On Sunday nights was Sunday school, which was divided into different age groups. Our group met in the youth pastor's office to study specific passages in the Bible. This one-on-one version of church was where I was able to truly speak out when the cracks started to form in my faith. I flickered between being disengaged to unleashing my frustration on my peers. It helped that I would bring Ritalin that a boy with ADD gave me at school. I'd hole up in a stall in the church washroom and snort it off my religious books, then waltz back into Sunday school and proceed to break down what I saw as the flaws in the church's views as articulately as I could while high as a kite. The Ritalin gave me the courage to speak out against the church. I have a vivid memory of yelling, "You're all indoctrinated!" at my youth pastor when he was trying to reason me back toward Jesus. I even threw a boy I knew into a bookcase for touching my hat. I had a lot of rage and nowhere to put it.

The last time I went to the church of my childhood was a Saturday night. I was visiting my mother right after my father had moved out of the house. My sister and I had pre-mixed vodka into a bottle of Mountain Dew and were half-way to drunk by the time we stepped out of the car in the church parking lot. We polished it off in the bathroom and decided it would be wise to sit away from our mother during the service. That night in church I felt a warmth that I hadn't felt in a really long time. The music was beautiful and compelling. Even though I had spent that last year at church with my arms crossed and refusing to sing along, now I poked my sister, giggling, and told her that we should join in. So together we sang in a perfect falsetto at the top of our lungs to every song. I imagine if my mother had noticed us, she would have been pleasantly surprised. It was an outpouring all right, but not the kind of spiritual rebirth that would lead us back to God. It was more like the grand finale in our religious lives. Soon after, my mother switched to my grandmother's church so she could leave her memories—of my father being a deacon there, and my brother Jack's funeral—in the past. It's likely she never found out that we were drunk that night, but I think she knows now that she'll never hear my sister and me sing at church again.

Becoming Nothing

WHEN I WAS NINE our father moved the family into a huge house in the suburbs because he thought it would make him look rich. It turned out to be more than we could afford, and my mother ended up taking care of several children in order to bring in some cash and keep the consequences of my father's spending at bay. On any given day, the house was alive with the noise of eight or ten kids in addition to our family.

One day when I was a bit older, though, I arrived home earlier than usual, and the house was hushed. No banging toys. No screaming. John, the baby who was born when I was ten, must have been napping. My other brother and sister would be home later because they went to a different school. I found my mother sitting at the table in the dining room. It was so rare to see her sitting down. She looked up and said, "I had to cancel babysitting today. Your father is in the hospital again. He stopped taking his pills." She took a breath. "I'm leaving him. I don't want you kids to have to live like this. It's not fair."

I had become used to the stunned feeling that came over me, but that never made it pass any faster. My parents were getting a divorce? I mumbled something to her, grabbed a snack in the kitchen, and floated up to my room. By then, my childhood loyalty to my father was almost gone. His ever-expanding illness was now encroaching on me. He had started to scream directly at me instead of behind a closed door at my mother. In my room, I lay on my back and stared at the ceiling. Trying to think made me feel very light.

That night our phone rang many times. It was my aunts, my father's sisters, calling to tell my mother that they supported her and that they were praying that Jesus would give her the strength to see that their marriage was sacred. They said that my father was just a very sick man. It was her duty as a wife to stick by him. It was all there in the vows she took. My vision of our family's life without him folded into itself before it could fully form as I sat on the stairs listening to my mother talking to my aunts. She wanted to believe them.

We all wanted to believe that he was just sick and that God had a plan for us. Believing this would make my father's illness the monster that had done all the things I hadn't even begun to remember; the things that hung like a thick blanket over me and made me feel like I was the ugliest person who had ever lived. But after hearing my aunts' advice repeated by her friends at church, my mother crumbled. My father came home from the hospital just like he had the time before.

That's when I stopped eating. I never made a conscious decision to do so. I just opened up my lunch one day at school and thought, *I wonder if I could go without eating this?* The challenge stretched on for weeks. I would try to eat the absolute minimum amount of food without getting caught. At dinner, I took as little food as I could and pushed it around my plate to make it look like I ate more than I did. It excited me that I could decide something for myself; it was a secret mission that no one knew about and no one could stop. Sometimes I fantasized about everyone finding out and eventually I'd get to be a guest on *Oprah*. I would tell her the story about my dad and she would listen carefully and with great sympathy.

But that never happened and soon starving myself wasn't enough for me. I couldn't feel anything anymore, and started cutting up my arms and legs, challenging my body to feel something. I wore long sleeves and pants to cover up the neatly organized scars all over my body. This left me vulnerable, because it proved that I was as unstable as my father said I was.

Soon after, I met the boy at junior high who had been diagnosed with ADD. He had a crush on me, and used to follow me around at lunch hour. I gave him the cold shoulder until one day he handed me a folded-up piece of paper. The Ritalin was inside it. "I haven't been taking it so I can be more fun," he said. "You should crush it up and snort it."

And so I did: back in my room at home, I crushed up one of the the pills with my piggy bank and clumsily snorted it through rolled-up paper for the first time. At the dinner table that night, my mind was buzzing. I did my usual routine of eating a tiny bit and then pushing the rest of my food around on the plate. I could barely sit still through our father's Bible reading, and as soon as he was finished, I raced back to my room.

I crushed and snorted another pill and then wrote a song. The song was good. Ritalin had made me a genius. I could see things so clearly; it allowed me to draw huge pictures and write long poems. I could feel things. I became friends with the boy who gave me the pills, and told him that I liked the comics he would draw for me of people with swords through their bodies and heads, and he kept handing me folded-up pieces of paper. We went on to attend the same high school together, where our routine continued.

I couldn't run away from home in a city that was so expansive and cold. You could run for half an hour and not even get to the end of your own neighbourhood, and all of the neighbourhoods looked the same, so it didn't really feel like escaping at all. Instead I was trying hard to become nothing, eating only a granola bar during the day and then hardly anything for dinner. I would crush up Ritalin at school to write music and tests, and then get the shakes when I came down or ran out. Once, thinking I was cold, all of my new high school friends piled their jackets on top of me as I shook uncontrollably on the lawn outside McDonald's. When I was on the wrestling team, I managed to drop a weight class by eating nothing but iceberg lettuce for two weeks and then on the day of the weigh-ins, jogging for ten kilometres with a garbage bag tied over my torso to make me sweat more. But I knew that losing that weight wouldn't help me wrestle. I never won a match, although I enjoyed the self-control it took to drop down to ninety-five pounds.

When my mother let me move to my grandmother's, I started trying to eat food again, if only because my grandmother had worked so hard to prepare it. At dinner she went out of her way to cook things she knew I liked, and then she and I would sit at the table alone while my uncle ate in his room so he could watch TV. She also packed me huge lunches that I found hard to throw out. Being taken care of made me feel better, but I discovered that I had established a pattern of behaviour that would be difficult to break. Every day was a fight to eat anything at all. Before I moved in with my grandmother, I thought that all I had to do was get away from my father and then everything would be perfect. The truth, however, was that once he receded from my life, I continued to want to disappear because I felt like he was still close at hand.

The night that my mother and my brothers and sister showed up at my grandmother's house, they had escaped my father for the last time. That evening, my mother and I had a conversation in the dark. "When I told him I was leaving, your father said that Uncle Mike abused him," she said.

"Oh ..." I trailed off without really responding. *Abuse?* I thought. *Even if he was lying about it, does that mean he could be capable of abusing people himself?*

And then it all washed over me. The memories that I had crumpled up and stuffed far from my waking thoughts. Pieces of them crawled back under my skin and filled me with terror. *Maybe he had abused me?* I turned into stone.

The next thing I remember, I was standing behind my grandmother's garage and smoking, not thinking about getting caught. I was trying to put myself back together. How could I have not thought of this until now? I had felt it without knowing it. Was this the reason why I had wanted to die since I was eleven, why I couldn't eat or feel? It was like suddenly looking down at myself and noticing all of the painful injuries that I had been too shaken, too unwilling to see. They covered my entire body. They lived inside every bone and vein.

I called Rena, who had recently agreed to be my girlfriend, and told her.

"Are you going to tell your mother?" she asked.

"No. She's been through too much already," I replied. "What are people supposed to do when they figure this kind of thing out?"

"I don't know," she said. "But whatever you decide to do, I'll be there with you."

I had grown up and around everything that had happened and now there was no way to separate myself from it, but I felt a resolve growing inside of me. I didn't want to turn into nothing now that I knew why I felt that way. I had refused to live in a house with my father and now I was willing to do anything to get my body back. No matter how long it took.

Music Saves

WHEN I WAS FIVE, I started piano lessons with a woman named Belinda who discovered that I had double-jointed thumbs. She noticed that when I tried to reach certain keys, I would pull my thumb out of its socket. I don't remember learning to read music, just as I don't remember learning to speak. I enjoyed playing the piano, but I was not a protégé by any means.

I played a song called "The Sewing Machine" with both hands at my first recital. My mother had put me in a black dress with white leotards and black patent leather shoes. Before it was my turn, I watched the other students perform their songs. Some of them were much older than me, and much better at playing the piano. My entire family was there to see me. When they called my name I stood up, but my knees were shaking. As I crossed the stage, one of my shoes slipped and I did the classic slapstick fall. Some of the children in the audience, and even some of the parents, couldn't help but laugh. Belinda rushed over and helped me up. I tried to hold in my tears and limped over to the piano bench, mortified. Staring down at the white and black keys, I started playing. Luckily I had memorized the song, so when tears began to fall down my face I kept going, even though I couldn't see the music anymore. The song was less than two minutes long, but I kept repeating to myself over and over: "I will never play music in front of people again."

Still, once I learned to read music, there was no stopping its presence in my life. When my grade three teacher, Mrs. Crown, found out that I could read music, she recruited me to play the hand bells. I felt a lot more comfortable performing when there were eight of us in a row, gripping the bells with our tiny white-gloved hands. I didn't really have to read music because I only had two notes, one in each hand. Mine were the high F# and G on the treble clef. All I had to do was count the notes that the others played and confidently swish my bells out with my arm and then back to my body whenever I saw one of my notes circled in red on the sheet in front of me.

When I was nine, a woman named Karen Spencer took over our church children's choir. She seemed to have two goals in mind: to cast her own children as leads, and to put on the most intricate musicals our church had ever seen. Being in the children's choir was mandatory. I enjoyed singing but would have preferred to retire from acting after I played the Virgin Mary in a church play as a toddler. Anyway, I never sang loud enough in public for anyone to hear, and spent choir practices mouthing the words and staring down at my feet. For her first production, Karen chose a musical whose lead character was named Psalty the Singing Songbook. It took the audience through three Bible stories to find the meaning of love, which was of course Jesus dying on the cross. There were so many songs in the musical that Karen had to look outside of her immediate family to fill all of the solos. By default, she gave one to me. It was a verse in a song that was set to the tune of "Louie,

Louie," to be performed during the story about Moses. At home, I would sit cross-legged in my room, look down at the music sheet, and practice: "Pharaoh, Pharaoh, ooh baby, let my people go."

On the night of the performance, all of us were dressed in our parents' interpretation of Old Testament garb. We had bare feet, bathrobes, and towels tied with ropes around our heads. My mother had made sure that I wore leotards just in case part of my legs showed from under my bathrobe. Karen's teenaged son played Psalty and was costumed as a huge songbook with his face painted blue. During most of the show I was part of the chorus and followed obediently as Karen directed us. Under the hot lights I grew warmer, and my legs started to sweat, then itch, in my leotards. I tried discreetly to scratch them, but that only made me want to scratch them more. By the time my solo came, my legs were on fire. I tried to get through it without scratching, but I couldn't. I watched myself on videotape later, struggling to get the notes out in a wavering voice, and reaching down to scratch between every line. That was the first and last solo Karen ever gave me.

In grade eight, I started my first guitar class. There were thirty of us students sitting in rows with nylon string guitars. The teacher was the same one I had for junior high band, where I had spent the whole previous year playing trumpet on Bryan Adams songs and the theme to *Jurassic Park*. Somehow thirty guitarists all playing at the same time produced a more cacophonous sound than the brass section in band. Muddled versions of "Ode to Joy" rang through the hallways as we struggled to learn our first tunes. They included cool new songs I had never heard of before, like "Let It Be" and "Imagine." I would go home after school and practice our guitar assignments for two or three hours every night so I could play them well the following day. I found playing guitar absorbing; I would forget about everything else around me as I practiced the songs over and over again. One day, I decided to try to sing "Stand by Me" and play guitar at the same time. My voice started out weak and my guitar sounded clunky, but by the end of the song it was recognizable. I started over and played it again. Elated that I could play a song, I decided to write my own.

At that time, I was still a Christian. The only record I'd ever seen my parents buy was Amy Grant at the Christian bookstore downtown, when I was still too short to reach the vinyl stacks in the music section. I listened to Christian teen heartthrob Michael W. Smith, and my cousins and I did the running man to Christian rap group DC Talk. So it's not surprising that the subject of most of my early songs involved Jesus. He was all I knew. When my youth pastor discovered that I played guitar, he invited me to play in the rock band at Friday night youth group. I learned how to jam along by ear and play bar chords. We played pop songs, but adapted the lyrics for the Lord's purposes. Our version of "Surfin' Safari" went, "Come on baby, Surfin' the Lord. Come on baby, Surfin' the Lord."

It was around this time that I met Carla, the youth group leader whom I had a crush on. Each week I would write a new spiritual song and play it for her on Friday. I would always perform in one of the back rooms of the church, and I discovered that if I played songs about Jesus, the other teenagers would circle around me and listen. This was the first form of popularity that I ever experienced. I bought my first tape recorder with money I made from babysitting when I was twelve, and I'd make Carla tapes of the songs I wrote, recorded in my room. Soon others started requesting copies, so I made more and started selling them at church, hand-drawing cross designs on the covers and writing out the song titles with different coloured ballpoint pens.

My tape recorder was not only a spiritual tool. While I used it to record my own Christian contemporary songs, it also had a radio, and I discovered secular music by quietly playing the rock stations with my ear next to the speaker. I often fell asleep spooning it in my arms. There was a world beyond junior high school, church, and my house, and it began to transport itself into my room through the radio. A new picture of reality was beginning to emerge in my head, and it grew with every new song I heard on the radio. There was something in secular music that made it sound better than anything I had ever heard before. The wild and driving howls of the devil's music were far more compelling than the repetitive electric pianos in songs about abstinence. I wasn't sure I wanted to spend eternity in hell, but it didn't take me long to decide that I wanted to spend my teenage years with the devil. I would wait until my favourite songs came on—like Nirvana's "Heart-Shaped Box" and Pearl Jam's "Jeremy"—and tape them, often missing the opening chords or running out of tape and having only half the songs to listen to, over and over.

I listened to Nirvana before Kurt Cobain was found dead in his garage, but it was only then that he became an obsession for me. My parents subscribed to *Time* magazine, and when the issue with him on the cover was delivered to our house that week I squirrelled it away in my room, cutting out the pictures and taping them to my wall, which eventually became covered with his photos. I managed to sneak all five of Nirvana's albums past my parents into my room through several covert missions to the mall. Kurt Cobain's music was full of unapologetic pain and anger. I discovered my own pain and anger by listening to it. While my church and family encouraged us to rejoice even when absurdly tragic things happened, grunge allowed me to express the unfairness of life. To me, Kurt Cobain was the personification of the rage I felt. I wanted to be him.

My grandma gave me an old green cardigan that had been hanging in her closet when I was visiting one day. I wore it all the time, with ripped jeans and flannel shirts, except on Sundays when I would have to sit in church in a dress, my hair hanging in my face and the ear buds of a Discman hidden from view. Grunge music made church more bearable.

I spent hours every night writing songs and practicing guitar, and I also took it to school and played it during lunch hour. Music became everything to me. When my father grounded me for months for defying him, he let me keep my guitar; hiding in my room, I felt like it was all I needed to survive. I remember writing a song once while he banged on my door threatening to take me to the hospital; I could barely hear him. Later on when he stopped living with us, I used music to hide from my memories. Nothing could touch me when I was writing or singing a song.

As I started my haphazard escape from the church, my music was right there with me. My faith would ebb and flow as I tried to realign my perspective. At first I saw rock music as the devil tempting me, but in time church became the thing I needed to escape. It was drummed into my head that without the church, I would have no spiritual protection. I imagined this as being the same as a spaceship alone in the void, pelted by debris. At youth group they would get us to close our eyes and then describe hell to us: "Imagine the most painful thing you've ever felt; now multiply that by a million and you would still not be in as much pain as hell. Hell is so horrible that if you saw even a glimpse of it, you would die from shock." And hell is where they thought people who liked grunge music belonged.

In senior high, I escaped the solitude of my junior years by playing songs in the hallway to make friends. It worked the same way it did at church, except that now I was singing about being angry instead of rejoicing over Jesus. There were plenty of others around who could identify with that. When my parents divorced, I took over the basement of our new duplex to make recordings on my four-track tape recorder. I borrowed instruments and made tapes that I would take to school and sell just like at church, for five dollars apiece. One day I heard that a famous singer from Calgary was coming to talk to my sister's singing class, so I went to see her. She was very funny and talked about golfing with another Canadian singer that my family always listened to at Christmas. After it was over, I went to the front of the class and nervously handed a tape to her, mumbling that I had made it myself. I was star-struck. I had seen the Juno Awards she had won on display in a downtown store that she co-owned. The tape I made for her was called "Androgynous Fool." I had added a zero to the number of available copies on the side, so it would look like I had made fifty instead of just five. The songs were about wanting to escape and not being able to come out as gay. After school that day, I went to work at the gas station. When I came home, my mother and sister were running around the house excited, saying over and over, "She called you! She called you!"

My sister had talked to her. She said she liked my tape and that she would call back to talk to me. After all of the chaos it took to get my father out of our lives, this was one of the first really good things that had happened to my family. I waited for two days for her to call back. When I answered the phone, she asked me some questions. I told her I was seventeen and that yes, I did write all of my own songs. She told me that she really liked my tape and that I should keep writing. Then she said something that took me by surprise: "You know, you should come out to your mom."

I paused, wondering if I should deny her assumption and say that I had made up the gay stuff. I wanted to tell her how homophobic and religious my mother was, that she would rather lose her children than change her views. I wanted to tell her that I was terrified that someone would tell my girlfriend's parents that we were queer and that I would lose her forever, and how scary it was to walk around at night in my neighbourhood, but I choked it all back. "Yes, I should do that someday," I replied shakily, tears welling in my eyes.

A few teachers at school had expressed mild concern when they found out that some students were terrorizing the queer ones; they treated our identities as a mere misfortune. But this singer was the first adult who ever told me to stand up for myself and to be proud of who I was. She provided some necessary fuel to get me through the difficult years that followed by making me feel special. Now when I play the tape I gave her fifteen years ago I cringe at how young I sounded, but I can also hear the terrified teenager that she heard. I can see what made her pick up the phone.

Change Your Name

WHEN OUR MOTHER WAS pregnant with our brother Craig, she used to play a game with my sister and me. Every morning as soon we woke up, we would run to the kitchen and get some saltine crackers and apple juice. The night before, our mother would make sure the box of crackers was at the edge of the counter where we could reach them. Then we would sit next to her bed on the floor and have a picnic breakfast while she ate them still lying on her side. I broke the crackers into tiny pieces and chewed on them while my sister would suck on them until they were soggy. Then we would wash them back with the apple juice from plastic cups. My mother couldn't stomach anything else. "It's what the baby wants to eat," she would say.

I don't remember our mother leaving the house to give birth to Craig, but I do remember her being gone. While she was in the hospital, our father cooked our meals; one day, he burned the scrambled eggs, but made my sister and me eat them anyway, and yelled at us when we cried about it. Later, though, he felt bad and took us out for pizza right before we went to the hospital. He told us not to tell anyone. We licked the tomato sauce off our faces under the hospital lights and never told our mother about the burnt eggs.

Our new brother Craig was named after our father because he was the first boy to be born in the family. When we brought him home from the hospital, I realized that I was going to be the oldest of three. My sister and I were too close in age for me to think of her as a baby, but Craig was tiny and bald except for a very thin layer of hair. He would lie in his crib throwing up on himself or crying when he wasn't sleeping. I had started kindergarten two months earlier and was the smallest in my class. After my days at school feeling terrified of everyone around me, it was nice to come home and tower over Craig. Later, as he learned to speak and walk, he became a better sidekick for me than my sister. He was willing to do pretty much anything I wanted, and he believed anything I said.

One early December when Craig was five, he still had leftover Halloween candy because he was allowed only one piece a day. Being older, I had been left to manage my own supply, and it had been gone for weeks. I crawled under his bed one night right before his bedtime, laying there undetected as I listened to our mother tuck him in and say his prayers with him. I heard the door close and waited for a few minutes until I thought Craig must be half asleep. Then I whispered in a ghostly voice:

"Craig…"

I heard him shift above me, so I did it a couple more times.

"Craig… Craig."

"Yes," he finally responded.

"This is your conscience." I waited to see if he was buying it.

"Yes," he said.

"It's really important…" I paused for effect. "… that you give all your Halloween candy to Rae." I instantly knew I had taken it too far.

He leaned his tiny face over the side of his bed and saw me. "Rae!"

I rolled out from under his bed and ran giggling out of his room. He ended up giving me some candy anyway. Even when I was picking on him, he liked the attention.

I grew impatient with Craig while he was trying to learn how to ride a bike. The day my parents took the training wheels off, I decided that if he could go faster he would be able to stay upright.

"Craig, come with me!" I pushed his bike up the hill by our house and he followed.

"Get on," I instructed.

"Okay," he said, too trusting to protest.

"Just keep the handle bars straight and your feet on the brakes," I said, motioning to the pedals, which had back-brakes on them. I tapped him on the helmet, steered him in the right direction, and then let go. He sped down the hill, seeming to stay upright.

"Yay, Craig!" I called out. But my yelling must have thrown him off because the bike started to shake. He took a hard right and careened full speed into one of our neighbour's rose bushes. I ran down the hill and pulled him out. His arms and face were all scratched up, but he was smiling.

"You did it!" I said. He never told on me.

Throughout our childhood, I couldn't understand why Craig got to wear suits to church with his hair slicked down with a comb while I had to wear dresses. Hadn't my parents noticed that I was better at being a boy than he was? I was way more talented at building forts and climbing trees. My father would often refer to him as the man of the house, but Craig was never quick to take on that role. He was quiet, gentle, and loved animals, and didn't seem the least bit interested in becoming the kind of man that my father was. He would nervously crack his knuckles whenever it seemed like it was time for him to show his strength or skills as a boy.

When my father was put on a strong dose of anti-psychotics and spent most of his time sleeping, I took on the job of distracting my brother. It was best for us to stay outside and away from our father's sleeping form on the couch. Craig and I would play road hockey with the boys from our neighbourhood while my sister was inside playing with John the baby. We made Craig the goalie because he wasn't into fighting for the ball. He would stand in front of the goal wearing his foam road-hockey pads, sometimes wringing his hands when the game moved away from him to the other end. I was the oldest and bigger than all the boys. I would run up and down the street body-checking them and taking illegal slap shots above my waist. I had something to prove. Whenever I scored, I would drop my stick and cheer.

When I moved to my grandmother's to escape my father, it meant leaving the rest of my family behind. I couldn't afford to think about what it was like for my brothers and sister when I left; all I could think about was my own survival. Thinking about my siblings living across town in a house with my father made me feel sick to my stomach, and then … nothing at all.

When Craig and the family visited me at Grandma's, I wanted to let him in on my secrets even though I was beginning to think of myself as an adult. Once when he was hanging out with me in my room, I got him to smell some green stuff in a bag. "What is it?" He asked.

"Tea," I lied.

"It smells like a skunk," he said, wrinkling his nose.

When I was sixteen, after our father was out of the house for good, we packed all of his stuff in the van so he could drive it to wherever he was headed. It sat in our garage for a month. Our father was slow about leaving and fought the divorce at every step. He knew our mother didn't have any money and he wanted to weaken her by forcing her to spend it on legal bills. He fought for full custody of the boys and lost because the therapist he had originally forced me to go to advised against us having too much contact with him. It didn't take long for his name to become forbidden in our house.

When I moved back to our mother's house, I was able to spend a lot of time around Craig again. One afternoon while we packed to move into the duplex that was a quarter of the size of the house we had lived in before, Craig and I were out front taking a break. Somehow we got on the topic of our father. "I hate him," I seethed. "I'm glad he's gone. I don't care if we have to move into a tiny house. Anywhere is better without him."

I looked at Craig. He looked sad.

"What's the matter?" I asked.

"It's just that I hate him too ... but I have the same name as him," he whispered.

"I know. That sucks," I said. "You know you could change it, right?"

"Really?" he said, his eyes lighting up.

"You have two middle names. Why don't you pick one of those?" I said. "Let me try them out on you ... Hello, Robert!"

He shook his head. I tried the other one. "Hello, Phil!" I said, grabbing and shaking his hand. He smiled.

"Okay. We'll call you Phil, then. Let's go inside and tell everyone."

The look on his face melted my heart. Of course he wanted to change his name. None of us called him by our father's name again. That was the beginning of us all starting over. It was the first little sliver of our father that we pulled out and threw away. There were many more left, but getting started meant we were walking away from him instead of being pulled toward him. And that made all the difference in the world.

Second Coming

I WAS SITTING IN GRADE twelve chemistry class writing a test. The whole room was quiet except for the scratching of No. 2 pencils on paper. The test was multiple choice; I scanned the list of questions so I could answer the easiest ones first. I hadn't been able to sleep the night before, so there weren't many that seemed clear. The questions kept blurring in front of me.

Because I couldn't sleep, I'd spent the night creeping around our house. I went from room to room checking to see if my family members were in their beds, panicking when I couldn't make out their forms in the dark and moving onto the next room when I did. I became more agitated each time I repeated the pattern. After all, I'd been raised to believe that according to the Book of Revelation, Jesus could come back any day in the Rapture and that when He did, all Christians would disappear from the face of the earth, abandoning those who would be "left behind." When I left the church at the age of sixteen, I had crossed the divide to the ones left behind. I wasn't sure if I believed in God during the day, but in the middle of the night, it was clear that something was haunting me.

I couldn't shake the worry that I was going to be left behind in the Rapture. I was eight years old when I read the Book of Revelation for the first time; I read it from beginning to end, with its four horsemen of the apocalypse, the breaking of the seven seals, and the sign of the beast. It said that all of the water on earth would turn into blood and that it would also rain down from the sky.

My parents often made reference to the second coming of Christ when we talked about death. They would cite the part of Revelations that said that the faithful dead would rise to praise the Lord and would join Him in the sky. I pictured my grandfather and my brother flying out of their graves. It was comforting to them and terrifying to me.

At the beginning of the end of the world, there was supposed to be the sound of a trumpet in the sky, heralding the arrival of Jesus. I listened for that trumpet everywhere I went. It could have been a car driving past our house at night, or a plane flying overhead. Every sound I couldn't place was a trumpet. So one day when the classroom heater made a sound in the middle of my chemistry test, I again heard a trumpet. I started looking at everyone else in the room, worried that if I blinked they would all vanish. What if my parents were right? What if I was a sinner? I thought I was going to start screaming, but I knew an outburst would draw attention to my out-of-control thoughts. Whenever I grew close to asking for help, I pictured the hospital where I had visited my father when I was eleven. There was not a lot of help for anyone there. It was better to keep my fears to myself.

So I stood up and walked out of the class, down the empty hall and past the rows of lockers. I headed to the only place in the school where I felt safe, an empty stairwell. I used to sit there and quietly sing and play guitar when I had a spare period between classes. The door was the backstage entrance to the school theatre. Sometimes when I was singing, drama students would poke their heads out to see where the sound was coming from. This time I was too worked up to think of getting my guitar. I sat alone, pressed up against the wall, trying to slow down my thoughts. I knew there was no God, so why was I still afraid?

It began the moment my father was out of the picture. I was at my grandma's house lying on the couch and suddenly my whole body went numb. I was convinced that I was dying. But there was always a layer of reality in which I knew my thoughts were illogical. It didn't make sense to me that freedom from my father would contain so many panic attacks. I thought I was going to have a new life where I didn't have to fight with him everyday, but now I fought eternal damnation within myself.

When I got home after the test that day, I went to my room and lay down on my bed. *I've got to stop this*, I thought. The plywood wall of my basement bedroom was covered in a collage of pictures that I'd cut out of magazines. Everything looked two-dimensional and hazy. *Go away!* I yelled at Jesus. *Be real!* I yelled at my room. Nothing seemed present to me anymore. Everything was coated in a thick layer of foreboding.

Every time the furnace in the basement went off, it sounded like a gunshot. This time it snapped me out of not being able to move. I stood and picked up a picture of Rena, my girlfriend. I put it on top of my Bible and took a picture. Then I threw my Bible into the garbage. Not wanting my mother to discover this extreme act of blasphemy, I took my garbage out to the pail in the backyard, looked up at the sky, and dropped it in. I had made my decision.

My father was gone. Our new home, half of a duplex, was dark brown against the huge, blue sky. I had the urge to look for blood raining down somewhere but resisted. I had picked a side. From now on I was going to talk myself out of these impulses. I was a non-believer, and no matter where I ended up for eternity, at least life itself would no longer be hell.

With a Little Help from Grunge

AS A TEENAGER, I NEVER considered myself grunge, but I still wanted to stand out. When I got dressed in the morning, I thought like the anger I felt inside would boil over and onto my outside. By grade nine, my V-neck vests and white Guess jeans failed to get the point across, so I started to dress all in black, ripped-up clothing. Looking at my frayed and oversized clothes in the mirror, I felt that I was getting closer to being cool. So I took it further.

I tried to learn how to smoke. It was hard work; first, I had to find cigarettes. I smoked my first one in the bushes at a church picnic. My church friend who really liked AC/DC gave it to me when I caught her smoking and asked if I could join her. After that, I mostly found them on the ground. My sister had started smoking with her friends from school. She and I would spend our summer afternoons combing the ground at the nearby C-Train station. One day we smoked so many stale butts that she threw up on the bus on the way to our grandmother's house. But by then we were both addicted and it was too late to quit. We started buying them from the older kids at school or at the one store in downtown Calgary where they didn't ask for ID. Besides addiction, there was also dizziness to contend with. Too many cigarettes made me feel like I was on a ship in a storm. But at least I was cool, even though I often struggled to keep myself from weaving along Calgary's land-locked city sidewalks.

My sister and I were able to keep our habit from the family. A lot of my aunts and uncles smoked, but I knew our grandmother and mother would be crushed if they found out that we did. If we wanted to smoke when they were around, we would leave the house under the guise of going to get a Slurpee at 7-Eleven. Smoking is not a seasonal activity, and I'm surprised they never questioned our need for the icy drink when the temperature outside was minus twenty-five. At 7-Eleven we would buy a Slurpee and then go around the back of the store behind a dumpster, where we were hidden from view except for little puffs of smoke that looked like they came from two tiny chimneys. Afterwards we would soak ourselves with a bottle of CK1 cologne that I carried in my jacket pocket and walk back home. When I think about it, I'm surprised that I fooled myself into thinking we were hiding anything. Even so, we didn't get in trouble, and the cigarettes made me look a lot tougher. One afternoon when I was standing outside the mall with one hanging out of my mouth, a lady shouted over her shoulder at me, "Delicate. Really delicate."

The day I started smoking publicly, I made a lot of smoke friends at school. They were easier to rebel with than my band friends had been. They drank beer and smoked pot instead of playing the clarinet or oboe. We had something in common besides cigarettes, too. A lot of them were bullied for being weird. The thing about Calgary was that boys didn't really need to be gay to get called "faggot." You only had to do something a little out of the ordinary, like grow your hair long or play the acoustic guitar. And if you were a girl, all you had to do was cut your hair short or stand up to boys and you would be called a dyke. There was one punk boy at school who had green hair; in grade ten he got beaten up so much that he transferred to the downtown school after a few months. There was danger in being different and there was safety in numbers. That's why the straight kids who were grunge were treated the same as the gay kids. We were all fags in the eyes of our school.

After school and on weekends, my smoke friends and I would spend all of our time together driving around in cars borrowed from their parents. We loitered in parks and alleys, and poured stolen booze into our Big Gulps. Sometimes we would even hang out with college kids who went to art school, which made me feel older than I was. But once at a party, just as I started to feel like I was blending in, a girl asked me, "What are you for Halloween … Obnoxious?"

I don't think we were searching for our adult selves because growing up felt like something that was never actually going to happen. So we tested the limits of our suburban lives without ever trying to escape them.

Our antics continued even after high school was over. One night after graduation, we decided to break into an outdoor public swimming pool because we were hot and some people we had met at the bar that night had done it before. My friend Micah drove us there in his big white boat of a car. We climbed over the two-storey fence and dropped to the ground. In my underwear, I ran and did a cannonball into the pool. When the water went up my nose, it choked me just like it would have if we had gone swimming during regular hours. Why shouldn't we be there? No one else was using it. We forgot to be quiet and loudly showed off to each other.

"Hey Micah, check out how far I can swim under water!" I said before I plunged beneath the surface and held my breath, determined to stay under until my lungs felt like they were going to implode. I could see the blurry forms of the other swimmers lit up by the moonlight. I exploded out of the water expecting applause, but my eyes were filled with a blinding light and I could hear a loud hum from above.

"Dude, it's the cop helicopter!" I could hear Micah yelling as he was grabbing his clothes.

"Shit!" I screamed, spitting water out of my mouth.

I'd heard of the police helicopter, but I'd never seen it before. I pulled my waterlogged body out of the pool and lunged at my shoes. Everything moved slowly like I was still underwater. I threw my clothes over the fence and screamed at one of the boys from the bar to boost me over. As I fell from the top of it, I cut the palm of my hand on a piece of the fence that was sticking out. We ran across the field pulling our clothes back on and hopping on our half-on shoes.

When we got back to Micah's car, he drove slowly down the alley without headlights so we wouldn't attract attention. Every motion sensor light on every garage went off as we crept past. I hung my head out the window and saw that the sky was dark and quiet again. That's when we started laughing, first in quiet giggles and then uncontrollably.

Micah drove us to an all-night diner that was half-way between our houses. We slouched across from each other smoking and nursing weak, bottomless coffees. I looked at my cut-up hand and grinned. It was more fun to be chased when you brought it upon yourself. I leaned my head back against the booth with a self-satisfied grin. My wet underwear was soaking through my clothes. We sure showed them.

Sprint

WHEN I WAS FIVE, MY mother dropped me off at school after a dentist appointment. She was young then, twenty-seven years old, and had three children. As she pulled our little silver Datsun up to the curb, I blurted out the question that had been bouncing around in my head as we drove: "Mom, what's a fag?"

I had heard other kids using this word the day before at the playground. My mother paused and then launched into a speech about how fags were men who were gay, which meant that they were men who slept with men, and that lesbians were women who slept with women. And that it was sinful. And that they were going to go to hell. She then took a breath and added that God made AIDS to punish gay people. I slunk low in my seat, sorry that I'd asked a question that had upset her so much. I slammed the car door and ran into my school without looking back. I was careful not to bring it up again.

My mother had always been the fastest runner at school for her age. She'd also been a tomboy. One time she wanted to win a sprinting race so badly in high school that she couldn't stop at the finish line and ran into a wall, breaking her wrist. And when a boy chased her trying to kiss her in the fifth grade, she just turned around and chased him back. "You should have seen the look on his face when I turned around and he realized that I was bigger than him," she told me, laughing.

Her father, my grandfather, was a preacher in the little town of Bowden. She was the third of six kids in her family. Every Sunday my grandma would play music in the church and the children would sing along. They grew up in what used to be a liquor store. My mother says she was confused when they moved there; she thought it had been a licorice store and spent the first day looking for candy.

My grandfather was a philanderer, but like in any small town, his transgressions didn't stay secret for long. My grandmother endured his behaviour even when it became public knowledge, until he left her for a teacher. She raised her children by herself and eventually moved to Calgary with her two youngest who were still teenagers, working first for a bank and then an oil company until she retired.

My mother was furious at her father. She hated his new wife. She tells a story about going to his house and kicking down the door with her cowboy boots because she thought he was pretending he wasn't home. My mother's eldest brother Carl won't even speak to him, and ignored him at my brother Jack's funeral.

My mother helped raise her two younger brothers. They used to fight so fiercely that one of them threw the other through the front window of their house once; stunned for a moment, he then jumped out of the window and they continued the fight in the snow. She told me there were many times that she had to threaten to throw a rocking chair to calm them down.

She never talked much about it, but there was a period when

my mother gave up on the church, dropped out of high school, and started drinking. I only know of it because she was in a car accident when she was sixteen with a boyfriend who was driving drunk. Both of her front teeth got knocked out, and now she wears caps. She says she lost consciousness after suffering a concussion. "I could have never woken up."

It was a story she told often, about how the accident made her scared of being alone in the world and that it helped her to return to God. From then on she stopped her wicked ways and tried to be more obedient.

My mother told me more than once that all she had ever wanted to do in life was to have children. That's probably why she rushed into marrying my father when she was twenty. They met at church; she said he was charming. He played the saxophone and everyone liked him. She only found out he wasn't as nice as he seemed after they got married when he became controlling and abusive, but she couldn't break up her young family. She had five children with him, and stayed with him for almost twenty years.

I faced the truth that my father was abusive before my mother did and tried to make her see it, quietly at first and, when that didn't work, as loudly as I could. At the dinner table in front of him, I would pressure her. "Tell the truth," I said. "You don't love him."

Later, she told me that she wanted to agree with me but was too scared of him, although my outbursts helped her to realize that she had to leave him. So she secretly decided that she would leave him if he became abusive again. Which, he did, a few months later.

When my mother left my father, it was our chance to be a different family. This time we could build something without him controlling every part of our lives. When my father showed up at our new house unannounced, I chased him away with a rake as the rest of the family applauded me from the window. We were standing up to him together.

For a couple of months it seemed like I was going to live without so much fear. But that was the summer that I started dating Rena. She had been my best friend all spring during the last few times my father was hospitalized while I was living away from them. Then a shadow fell over everything again. When I moved into my mother's new duplex, I hid my relationship with Rena, knowing better than to look for acceptance. I hid all of my relationships from my mother until I moved out when I was eighteen.

I never talked to my mother about being transgendered. There didn't seem to be a point after the way things went when I came out as gay, when I called her from a pay phone after I moved out, drunk, and blurted out a list of my sins before hanging up: "I drink. I smoke. I'm gay."

We spoke of it again. When my sister Karen came out to my mother some years later, she asked, "Is everyone gay?"

My mother lost me even though she left my father to save her family. I know the divide between us will not be crossed unless she changes her entire belief system. It's unlikely that will ever happen, but sometimes I wish she could be as tough as she was when she

Art Hanger

FROM AS EARLY AS I can remember, during every federal election, my extended family's lawns hosted signs for their local Reform and later Conservative party candidates. My sister and I became particularly suspicious of our grandmother's consistent loyalty to her local Reform party MP, Art Hanger. One afternoon, as we sat on her front lawn gazing at the huge campaign sign with a black-and-white photo of him, we decided that the only explanation was that they must be romantically involved. In celebration, we took freshly trimmed pink flowers from her garden and decorated her long brown car with them wedding-style, giggling loudly. When she came outside to see what the commotion was, we chanted, "You love Art Hanger. Art Hanger is your boyfriend!" It made no sense, but we were convinced. She tried to explain that Art Hanger had a wife, but we knew that hadn't stopped our grandfather, her ex-husband, from having girlfriends, so were not dissuaded. The joke continued for years. We teased our grandmother relentlessly every time there was an election.

As a child I was the perfect candidate for a next-generation Conservative party member. At the tender age of ten, I was some-how able to simultaneously maintain my support for the death penalty while remaining pro-life, using well-memorized argu-ments that completely contradicted each other. Everything around me told me that the world was made up of two kinds of people:

the sinners and the saved. Conservatives and other people who voted Reform would be saved, while those in the Liberal Party were clearly sinners. It's easy to mark a ballot when it's explained as a matter of avoiding hellfire.

I am no longer a right-wing zealot, but I didn't drop my loyalties overnight. When Rena arrived at my grandmother's house for our last sleepover there, she noticed the election sign on the front lawn. (One of the advantages of living with Conservative relatives is their huge blind spot when it comes to queers in their midst, allowing for unlimited same-gender sleepovers.) When she got to my room, Rena looked at me with a disturbed look on her face and said the Reform Party sign out front was creepy. I laughed. "What, do your parents vote Liberal?" I asked, still convinced of the supremacy of my life-long convictions.

"Of course. If the Conservatives had been in power when my family immigrated to Canada, we might not have been allowed in. Their platforms are messed up and racist." She then proceeded to delicately explain why it was problematic for me to keep supporting the Reform Party if I was queer. Wide-eyed, I listened to her points and internalized them. That was the night that I parted ways with Reform Party leader Preston Manning and ended my stint as a gay conservative. I withdrew my blessing from my grandmother's imaginary affair with Art Hanger, and I began to build as much contempt for their alliances as she would have had for mine if she had figured out the motivation behind my many sleepovers.

I don't talk about politics with my family. I don't bring up my gender or sexuality either. The most I can do when I am around them is argue with their most pointed, off-base, bigoted comments—things I can't stand to let pass, which I will not repeat here. I have never been confronted by any of them about my obvious leanings, which are so perpendicular to theirs that when I was nineteen I even moved left of Alberta, to Vancouver. I assume that most of my family is living inside a comfortable cocoon of denial because they have left the obvious alone. My great-aunt, my grandmother's sister, is bolder, however. The last time I voted in Alberta, she was sitting in my grandmother's living room when I got back from the polling station. Given how overwhelmingly conservative Alberta is, voting there can be a moot exercise, but I did it because I wanted the candidate who ran for the left-leaning New Democrats to know that someone had voted for them. My great-aunt said, "I hope you voted the *right* way," and winked, repeating the statement until she was sure that I knew what she meant.

There is very little that I have in common with my family anymore, but once in a while there is some non-religious, apolitical moment that brings us together. One Christmas at my grandmother's house, I brought a lover with me from Vancouver under the well-worn guise of "best friend." It was late and we needed a ride to the C-Train. My cousin Casey offered. We said goodbye to my family and walked around the house from the back door toward Casey's purple low-rider truck, parked out front under a gentle dusting of snow. He had bought it with some of his first earnings as a welder on the oil rigs, a sign he had joined the ranks of my

Escape Hatch

I BROKE UP WITH RENA for the last time over the phone. She told me about how she had met a guy at a Take Back the Night March the evening before. He was a friend of a friend that we had casually met at Lilith Fair that summer. "He was running along the outside to keep up with me," she said. "He was waving a black flag."

I could hear the lump in her throat from the excitement. It was over.

I had a job at a gas station that wasn't going anywhere either. I thought that graduating from high school would mark the end of my feelings of being trapped, but I found myself working full-time at the gas station and spending even more time in the basement of my mother's house. To make matters worse, my best friend Micah was a supervisor at the gas station and made twice as much as me. He got to sit indoors with the sexually ambiguous cashier, and measure how much gas was left in the huge underground tanks. It seemed like a pretty cool job, but I overheard the manager explain once that women just couldn't be supervisors; they would be too vulnerable if the gas station was ever robbed late at night. So that was that.

What I really wanted was to be a professional musician. But how? Do I go to the heads of record labels and give them the 4-track cassette demos that I had been selling out of my lunch kit in high school? No. I was seventeen; it was time to be more grown-up about things. I pondered this while washing every single window on every single car that came into the gas station.

At work the day after Rena and I broke up, I washed the car windows methodically, without my usual zest. The cashier with the ambiguous sexuality noticed my mood and invited me to stack promotional pudding packs inside to cheer me up. During a lull, she asked, "What's wrong? You seem sad."

My lower lip quivered and my eyes brimmed with tears. "Nothing," I said. I was fighting to keep from sobbing, pretending to be immersed in the pudding packs that I was carefully stacking to form a pyramid. *So this is being an adult? Stacking pudding packs on your knees at a gas station?* I worked "feeling sorry for myself" into my job description for the rest of the day.

At the end of my shift I caught the bus back to my mother's duplex up the hill. Summer ends in Calgary on the day the northern wind decides to turn its attention back to the prairies. It was only the middle of September, but the leaves were already turning yellow and falling onto the brown grass. The grass is brown in Calgary most of the year, except, of course, for the green patches that appear after a grass fire. I looked out the window of the bus at Nose Hill Park, the biggest park in Calgary, and where the foothills begin. I wondered to myself what it would look like if someone set fire to it. Afterwards, for a brief moment, the whole thing would be electric green.

At home, getting past my mother without crying was hard. She hovered in the kitchen and wanted to talk about Crow River

College, where she was doing a year-long course in office administration. Our father had left her with nothing but four children after the divorce and she was determined to have her own career. She loved being in college and I was proud of her, but all I could do at that moment was shrug my shoulders and work my way towards the basement door.

I pounded down the stairs into the unfinished basement and ran toward my bed but couldn't quite make it, falling dramatically onto a pile of laundry on the floor. Tears rolled down my face and onto the clothes beneath me. *I could lay here forever*. The phone rang. My mother called down. I performed a miracle and pulled myself up.

"Hey Rae," the voice said. It was Terry, my friend who had been a year behind me at school. "I heard you broke up with Rena. I'm sorry … " I bit my lip. "I was wondering if you want to go to Fields Café tomorrow? It's your day off, right?"

Going out was the last thing I wanted to do, but I liked hanging out with Terry at the café, smoking cigarette after cigarette and making fun of each other. "Sure," I said. "That sounds like a good idea."

The next afternoon Terry pulled up in her dad's brown and tan '80s hatchback and I piled in.

"Where's your guitar?" she asked.

"Why?"

"You should ask to play a show at the café. You could audition." I rolled my eyes.

"The manager was there when you played the open mike a couple weeks ago. You can talk to him," she insisted as we pulled away from the curb.

There was always a thick haze of smoke at Fields Café. It attracted a mixed crowd of high school students, university students, and adults like. The orange and green walls were covered with colourful flower paintings that were for sale. Terry and I had been going to Fields for the last couple of years because no one cared there that all we did was chain-smoke and buy coffee refills on an hourly basis.

As we walked in, Terry turned to me and whispered, "He's here." The manager was standing behind the counter. But I wasn't ready to talk to him and made Terry get the coffee while I went to our favourite chairs by the window and lit a cigarette. Terry came over with two steaming cups. "Come on. Just ask him. I know he loves your music."

"Okay. In a minute," I grumbled. "How's school this year?" I asked, changing the subject.

"It's okay. Weird without all of you guys, but I'm just focusing on getting into university."

A knot formed in my stomach. Rena was going to the university. Almost all of my friends that I graduated with were going there. On the first day of Rena's classes, I went with her to the welcome concert on the school lawn. I felt like they were all flying away from me and soon Terry would too, but I didn't want to join them. I wanted to play music, but all I was doing was pumping gas and cleaning car windows. Suddenly I felt myself standing up and striding confidently toward the counter. I cleared my throat, which made the manager look up from his work. "Hi, Rae. What can I do for you?"

"Hi," I stuttered. "I was wondering … if I could play a show here sometime," I said, nervously putting my hands in my pockets.

"I think that's a great idea," he said. I felt my face start to glow. He opened his date book. "When do you want to play?"

"How about September 24?"

"You can play from eight until eleven. We'll pay you seventy-five dollars." That was almost twice what I made for a shift at the gas station. "You have to bring your own PA. Some people play acoustic, but your voice is so quiet, you should probably use a microphone."

"Sure, that sounds good," I said, trying to be casual as I turned to walk away. But as soon as I had my back to him, I was grinning from ear to ear. I had my first gig.

I spent the rest of the afternoon cutting letters out of a magazine for a poster and dubbing cassettes on my boom box in my room. The cloud from my breakup with Rena had lifted. For the first time in my life, I felt like I was moving forward toward something I wanted rather than running away from the things that I was scared of.

I put the poster in the window of Fields a few days later. I started practicing every moment I could, as soon as I got home from work and changed out of my gas station uniform. I used my four-track recorder as a mixer and my mother's stereo speakers from the '70s as my PA. Then I slowly put together the songs. Three hours was a lot of material, so I polished off a bunch of Paul Simon and Bob Dylan covers along with the songs I'd written in the stairwell at high school. My mother found out about the show after she heard me practicing. My family wanted to come see me, but aside from my sister, I didn't want them there. When I wrote songs, I didn't hide things about myself like I did at home. There was no way that I was going to come out to them before I moved out, and my songs would likely confirm any suspicions they had about me. This show was another thing I needed to hide from them, even though I longed to see my mother and my uncle John proud of me, in particular.

I got nervous as the date of my show approached. Finally, just as the last leaf of summer fell off the tree in our front yard, it was time. Terry pulled up in her dad's car and my sister and I dragged the stereo speakers, amplifier, four-track recorder, and guitar case out of my house.

By the time we got to the café, the sun had almost set. We hauled the gear in and I got to work putting together what I was trying to pass off as a PA system. My hands were shaking, my palms were sweaty, and I was cursing under my breath at the cords I was struggling to plug in correctly. *Why am I doing this?* I thought. *What if it's horrible? I wish Rena was here.* I scanned the crowd looking for her, forgetting that I had purposely not invited her. I had to do this without her. I sat back on a stool and picked up my guitar. This is what I wanted to do with my life and it was time to start. I looked down at the three-hour set list I had scribbled onto a piece of loose leaf. First song. The one about meeting Rena. *Here we go.*

Then I saw them. My sister, Terry, Micah, Terry's boyfriend Bud, and a lot of the grunge kids from high school were sitting at tables and standing at the back. There weren't enough chairs for them all. The café was full. My confidence swelled. I closed my eyes and began. At first I sang quietly, but got louder as I went. Even though my eyes were closed, I could see something that had never been there before. It was an escape hatch with light pouring out from behind it. When I sang, I moved towards it, floating, with my arms out in front of me. This was the way out. I wasn't sure how yet, but my voice would carry me forward to where I needed to be.

And then the song was over. I opened my eyes. The applause hit me hard, a thundering sound that I had never heard before. It was coming from my friends, but from strangers too. I felt myself grinning. The fire was inside me now.

Ice Blue Light

SMALL TALK AND TRAVEL are inextricably linked. The further I am from home, the more generalized my response to questions about where I grew up. Outside of Canada, whenever I mention Calgary, I often end up talking about the mountains instead of the prairies. The Rockies are only an hour away, and they're more impressive than anything else I can think of to talk about.

I grew up in several houses in different suburbs. Now when I visit, the colours of the beige aluminum siding and peach stucco make me sleepy when I see them. I still remember the long waits for buses that ran infrequently but would eventually take us downtown, where we would feel free to find some kind of meaning to our lives. Calgary is a relatively young city; even some of the houses in other cities that I've lived in are older than my hometown. Since moving away, I have been trying, yet failing, to grow a new history for myself. Many things happened to me in Calgary, and most of them are too painful to think about.

For this reason I don't think of Calgary when I'm homesick or feel overexposed. In those moments, I close my eyes and end up in the Rocky Mountains, at the foot of the Athabasca Glacier. As you climb past the markers of years showing where the ice has retreated, you can reflect on the passing years of your own life. A knee-level chain barrier is meant to block hikers from approaching the glacier, but most casually step over it. There are signs warning people about falling into one of the crevices. When some-one does, it swallows them whole.

I once visited the Athabasca Glacier as a child, although I can't remember when exactly. But I return to it in my mind whenever I feel unsteady. If you crouch below the glacier and look up into it, there's an ineffable blue glow. It's the light that travels through thousands of metres of ice before being spit out again on the grey rocks. I often find myself reflecting on that vibrant blue. It's a child-hood memory I can hide inside of instead of cower from. As far as small talk goes, I still haven't figured out a way to say that I was born in Calgary, but my heart lives in the blue glow under a frozen lake of water on top of a mountain in Alberta.

RAE SPOON is a transgender musician/writer/workshop facilitator originally from Calgary, Canada. Rae has been nominated for a Polaris Prize, toured internationally, and released six solo albums, the most recent of which is *I Can't Keep All of Our Secrets* (2012). Rae was published in the Arsenal Pulp Press anthology *Persistence: All Ways Butch and Femme*, edited by Ivan E. Coyote and Zena Sharman, composed the instrumental score for the National Film Board film *Dead Man*, and will soon be the subject of a National Film Board documentary. Rae lives in Montreal.

raespoon.com